APOCALYPSE LAW

By
John Grit

Also by John Grit

Feathers on the Wings of Love and Hate:
Let the Gun Speak
(Volume 1)

Feathers on the Wings of Love and Hate 2:
Call Me Timucua
(Volume II)

Apocalypse Law 2

<u>Chapter 1</u>

Nate Williams watched his four-year-old daughter die.

He sat by her bed and cried for thirty minutes before he could go to his son's bedroom to tell him. By the time he woke Brian, he was strong again.

Brian rubbed sleep from his eyes and blinked in the undulating glow of the kerosene lamp. He saw his father's unshaven, stony face looking down at him, holding the lamp out from his side at arm's length. The smell of the burning kerosene mixed with his father's unwashed body. He had been by Beth's side ninety-seven hours. There had been no time to take care of himself.

"She's not hurting anymore," Nate told him.

Brian's face tensed, holding back tears.

"It's a lot for you to take. You're not thirteen yet—and now you've lost your sister only two weeks after losing your mother. I'm sorry this world has been so cruel to you."

Brian sat up in bed. "What do we do now?"

"When it's daylight, we will bury her beside your mother."

Brian looked at his father for more than a minute. "It's cold." He sat on the edge of the mattress and crossed his arms.

"Get dressed and put some wood in the stove. I'll go out to the chicken coop and get some eggs. By the time we're through eating and cleaning up the kitchen, it will be almost light enough to start digging."

"I'll go out and pump some water," Brian said.

The father's eyes flickered in the lamplight and his voice rose. "No. You stay inside. It's about twenty out there."

"Dad, I'm stronger than…" He began to cry.

"It killed your mother, too. And the sickness is still a danger to us both. There's no need for you to be out there in the cold anyway." He turned for the door.

"Do you ever cry?"

Nate stood frozen in the doorway, his back to his son. "I never said you could not cry."

"I didn't say that." The boy wiped his face.

Nate turned, walked to a nightstand, and put the lamp down. "Come here." He held his arms open.

His son rushed to him, and they held each other as the boy's grief spilled out, his head more than a foot lower than the father's shoulders. He took more to his mother's side and had yet to show any sign of growing into a massive man like his father.

"I'm sorry," the father said. "I loved them both, but I couldn't save them."

"What about you?"

"I'll be okay as long as you are. You're all I have now. We two have to help each other make it." Nate's face was etched with years beyond his age, but his eyes were dry. He had done his crying; now it was his son's turn.

Out in the chicken coop, Nate gathered eggs in a two-gallon galvanized pail. He found only five. Something had been in the coop again. A raccoon? There was no sign that any of the hens were disturbed or attacked by an animal, no feathers or blood on the floor. No animal could have torn through the hardware wire, and the door was latched every night.

Nate walked outside and searched the ground's blanket of granular snow, holding the lamp high. They had suffered three severe winters in a row. Snow was uncommon in north Florida, but last winter it had gotten six inches deep. No one had heard of snow ever being more than a light dusting this far south. Florida sugar, it was called. Only his own tracks marred the white. Whatever it was had come and gone before the last snowfall. He went inside the house and locked the door behind him. When he came out of his bedroom, he had his heavy caliber revolver in a holster under his long coat. He kept the coat unbuttoned.

"You scramble the eggs while I get some water," he told Brian.

The hand pump lever resisted all but his last pound of upward pull and then broke loose with a sudden start. Nate nearly slipped on thin ice from water spilled on the concrete slab by Brian the afternoon before. After a dozen strokes, he had the five-gallon plastic bucket three-fourths full and bent down to grab the wire bale. His breath misted and hung in the still, cold air as he stood and looked around for sometime before walking to the front porch.

He put the bucket down and turned, standing there, searching the graying dawn. Nothing but snow-white trees on three sides. A twenty-acre field of white stretched toward the river. Brown straw from dead grass poked through the white powder around the edge near the tree line, where the blades of his tractor-drawn cultivator stopped when he plowed cornstalks into the earth after harvesting his last crop. The river misted; gray clouds of cold moisture hung patiently, waiting for the rising sun to warm the air and pull it up into the sky. Searching all he could see of his farm from the porch, he saw no movement. Whatever the egg thief was, there was no sign of it now. There was danger out there though; he could feel it in his guts.

Nate felt like a fool standing there presenting an easy target for anyone hiding in the brush on the far side of his field. But they had to tend the stock, pump water, and they had to eat. The farm was their source of food. They would starve if they just stayed in the house.

The scent of eggs cooking and fresh brewed coffee reached his nose before Nate got to the kitchen .

Brian looked up from the wood stove but did not speak. His eyes were red.

"We have to go on," Nate said. "You know that. There's no use in giving up." Nate noticed the eggs were burning. He grabbed a rag and took the pan off the stove, walked over to the table and pushed half of the eggs on one plate and half on another with a large spoon.

Brian stood by the stove, looking at nothing.

Nate sliced a loaf of bread and put four slices in the pan and the pan on the stove. "Get the butter out."

"There's not much left."

"We will churn some more later, when we have time. Might as well use it now."

Brian's chest rose, but he did not move for some thirty seconds.

Nate said nothing.

Finally, Brian brought the mason jar of butter over to his father, who used a knife to butter the sliced bread in the pan.

Nate looked at his son. "I need you to be strong. We have to go on."

Brian cringed as if he had just been struck a painful blow. "What's the point?"

"What's the point in giving up?"

"You said she's not hurting anymore. That sounds good to me."

"So you want to leave me alone?"

Brian did not answer.

"Well?"

Brian said nothing.

"I would never leave you, not if I had a choice. Your mother and sister fought like hell to stay with us. And I intend to fight to stay with you."

Brian wiped his face.

"It could be that the two of us have a resistance to the sickness. Look, life has handed you a bushel of pain. But you're young, with your whole life in front of you. There's no telling how much better it can be for you someday. This sickness and everything else will pass in time. We just have to survive until then."

"But they're gone. Dead. What about them?"

"I did all I could for them, and now I'm doing all I can for you." Nate stared at his son. "We're going to bury your little sister this morning, and then we're going to do our normal chores around here."

"What for? We're all dead anyway. Everyone is. Our neighbors, everyone."

"We two are not dead. Now stop that nonsense. I need you to help me through this as much as you need me."

"I mean there's nothing to live for."

"I'm living for you now." Nate put a thick slice of toasted bread on each plate. "People have to deal with losing their loved ones. Nearly everyone loses their parents and siblings, some lose their spouse and children too. I've lost everyone, everyone but you. That means you're all I have and I'm all you have. But you will have a wife and children someday. Then you will understand why I'm now living for you. And why you're wrong about not having anything to live for. There is a life for you…if you will just have the courage and strength to live it. Now let's eat."

Brian sat down and lifted some eggs to his mouth with a fork, then put it back on the plate. "I burned it."

Nate poured his son a cup of coffee. "Yes you did, but it's not bad. Put some hot sauce on it."

"I always use ketchup."

"We don't have any." Nate sipped his hot coffee.

"We could go into town and get some…and other stuff."

"Your eggs will be kind of cold by the time we get back."

"That's not what I mean."

"I know. Just eat. We have a lot to do today. The eggs aren't that bad. Here's some strawberry preserves to put on your toast." He pushed the jar closer for his son.

Brian did not touch it. "There is no God, is there?"

Nate looked at his son, his jaw set. He forced himself to swallow. "I don't know. Some say there is. You're mother believed. She was a good person, so she believed in good."

"I prayed Mom would live and she died. I prayed and begged Beth would live. I promised to do anything the Bible says we're supposed to do. But she died anyway."

"God never made a deal with anyone, Brian. Bargains are for the Devil and your soul." He looked away. "I'm sorry. Don't get cynical like me. You're too young for that. I don't know why people like your mother and little sister have to suffer and die. You're not the only one who prayed for them."

After breakfast, they went out to the barn and got shovels and a pick.

Nate stood by his wife's grave, looking. He searched the tree line, slowly sweeping, until he had searched the entire area with his eyes.

Brian watched. "What are you looking for?"

Nate shrugged. "Oh, I don't know. The egg thief I guess. I wish he would just come on in and introduce himself instead of sneaking around in the dark and stealing." He motioned for Brian to step back before he swung the pick, driving it into the frozen soil. It took him only seven minutes to loosen the two inches of frost covering a five-by-five foot area. He put the pick aside and started digging.

There was not enough room for both of them to work, so Brian watched as he leaned on his shovel. After a few minutes, he lifted his chin from the handle end and looked at his mother's grave. "You think she knows? Do you think Mom knows?"

Nate stopped shoveling and looked at his son. "Some would say Beth is already in her mother's arms and being welcomed to heaven." His chest rose and fell. "I don't know about after we die. Hell, I'm just doing the best I can about the here and now. Certainly little Beth was as good a little girl as there ever was. Don't you think?"

Brian looked away. Then he nodded. "She never did much wrong. She was better than me anyway."

"You dig a while, will you?" Nate stepped away.

After digging silently for several minutes Brian said, "It seems like we should put something on their graves to tell who they were."

"We will. I just haven't had time. Think about what you might want on them besides their names and when they were born and died. I'll have to chisel it out of wood, so don't make it too long."

"Wood will rot." Brian leaned on his shovel.

"I was going to use that 12 by 12 treated timber. We can drive a hole through, square it up with a chisel and put a smaller piece on, like a two-by-four, to make a cross."

"Okay."

"You rest a while. I'll dig."

Nate carried her out of the house. He had her wrapped in a blanket. She seemed even smaller in his massive arms.

Brian smeared his cheeks and turned away as Nate threw the first shovel load on her.

Nate began to shovel faster, with desperate force and speed. By the time he had her covered a few inches he was drained and fell to his knees, his chest heaving.

Brian turned and saw his wet face.

Nate looked down at the fresh soil. "It's the same as before—throwing dirt on someone you love takes a lot out of you." He pushed himself up from the ground and continued to shovel dirt on his little girl.

When finished, they stood over the mound of dark dirt for a few moments and said nothing.

"Well," Nate finally said. "We'll miss her. Miss them both." He picked up the pick and shovel and started for the barn with Brian following, carrying a shovel over his shoulder.

"I will milk the cow and feed it," Brian said. "Will you start on the crosses today?"

"All right. You can help after you've fed the chickens and shoveled the manure out of the stall."

It took Nate half an hour to saw through the 12 inch square pressure treated timber with a two-man logging saw. The usual strength he was accustomed to had left his shoulders and arms. He placed the two five-feet-long pieces on sawhorses and was using a hand brace to drill through one a foot from its end when Brian came in with an empty wheelbarrow he had just used to haul manure to a pile behind the barn. It would be used for fertilizer come spring.

Nate stopped drilling just short of going all the way through. It was the third hole he had drilled, all in line with one another. He put the brace down. "Grab the other end and help me turn it over so I can drill from the other side so it won't splinter the edge."

When he finished drilling the second timber, he used a wood chisel and hammer to chisel out the wood between the holes and enlarge and then square off the hole that was just large enough for a two by four inch board to slide through with a little hammering from a mallet.

Nate put the hammer and chisel down. "Now we have to think of what we want to put on them."

Brian looked away at nothing. "I haven't had time to think about it."

"You could have thought about it while you were working."

"I was…thinking about them."

"Okay. Let's go inside the house and maybe look in books or the Bible for something."

Brian sat at the dining room table and turned another page in his mother's Bible. "I don't know what I'm looking for."

"You're supposed to be looking for a short passage that would be fitting. Remember, there isn't much room and the letters should be large enough to read from a few feet away at least."

"Well, I can't find anything. This stuff is weird and hard to understand anyway. I don't think it's even English."

Nate read while he talked. "Look at that other book of poems then."

"This was Mom's?" Brian held a book in front of him.

"She read poems sometimes." Nate continued to read.

"What about this one?" Brian slid the book over so his father could see.

He shook his head. "Way too long. And I don't think it can be shortened without ruining it."

They continued to search the books. Thirty minutes later, Nate spoke. "Here is something. It's a little long, but I can chisel it into that last piece of timber and put it behind the crosses for both of them. We'll set it horizontal with those two granite blocks we have on each side of the driveway as pillars to hold it off the ground. We'll put their names and everything on the crosses themselves and this on the other timber."

Brian looked across the table at his father. "Those rocks are heavy. How are we going to move them?"

"I can get them on the utility trailer. We'll use the tractor."

"I wish you could chisel it into the stones."

"That would be better," Nate said, "but I don't have stone chisels and have never worked with stone. The wood will be good for now."

He read it to his son.

> The sun falls and the sun rises
> and so has she, ascended to heaven
> The sun shall fall again and the earth grow cold and dark,
> but she shall live forever in God's warmth and light.

Brian looked out the window. "Okay."

Chapter 2

"Why do we need a lock on the chicken coop?" Brian asked.

"Just a precaution. There are a lot of hungry people around nowadays, with all the troubles." Nate drove the last screw into the chicken coop door, firmly attaching a hasp to the wood. It would not stop a determined thief, but it would require him or her to make enough noise to alert Nate in the night.

"That's what you said about carrying your .44 and loading the shotgun and rifle. Just a precaution."

"It is. We haven't had any trouble yet. No one has been around."

"What about the barn? Someone might steal the cow."

Nate smiled at his son. "Good thinking. I will need that kind of help over the next few months."

"Oh hell. You already thought of it. That's why you found two old padlocks instead of just one. Don't treat me like Beth. I'm not little like she was."

"I wasn't. You're almost a man now. A father can kid with his son a little, can't he?" He punched Brian's shoulder lightly. "Let's get that lock on the barn. After that, you need to get your lever-action. We're going hunting this afternoon."

"Hunting?" Brian squinted in the sunlight. "I thought we were going into town to buy some stuff as soon as we got things squared away here. I don't like venison much anyway. Can't we buy something in town? We've never gone so long without going to town."

Nate put a screwdriver in his back pocket. "The same reason we couldn't take your mother and sister to the hospital."

"But the 3.police should have gotten the rioting under control by now. The hospitals might be open again too."

"No." Nate shook his head. "They're not going to open anytime soon. And the police are overwhelmed. Many of them died of the sickness just like everyone else."

Brian's face showed concern. "How long before things are normal?"

"Not for a while." Nate pretended to be busy checking the hasp and lock.

"Well, we need to go to the grocery store. I'm not going to live on eggs and venison forever."

"You like pork chops don't you?" Nate gave his son a strained smile. "Wild hogs were in the field last night. Tore up a half acre. I found where they went back into the woods and left a trail of corn to entice them back out. Maybe you can get a shot before dark. If not, the corn might bring a turkey out."

Brian sighed. "Okay, but we're going into town tomorrow, aren't we? There isn't much real food left."

"There's plenty of food for now. Let's go in and get ready. You'll need to dress warm. Stand hunting gets cold since we won't be moving and generating any body heat."

Nate came out of his bedroom with his M14 and jacked a round into the chamber, muzzle pointed at the ceiling.

Brian looked up from the kitchen table. He was wiping oil off his rifle. He stood and stuffed half a dozen 30/30 rounds into his right coat pocket. "I thought we're not supposed to have a loaded rifle in the house."

"That rule still goes for you."

Brian looked up at his father. "You're bringing your M14? Isn't it illegal to hunt with a twenty round magazine?"

"You're the one who's hunting. Besides, it's legal to hunt hogs on your own property with anything you want. They're not considered game animals, just trespassing feral livestock."

"But why do you have your military stuff? And you usually use your .44 revolver to hunt hogs 'cause the range is always so close."

Nate shrugged. "I thought I would get out my load-bearing harness and see if I can still carry all this in my old age. We won't be needing six extra magazines; no hog is that hard to kill. I just thought I would get it out and use it for old times."

"Dad, you carry stuff heavier than that every day. And you're not that old. You're only thirty-eight."

Nate's eyes lit up. "Thanks. But I just want to carry it today."

"Okay. It looks cool on you anyway. If you had an M4, you would look like you were in the Army again."

"Ready?"

"Yep." Brian started for the front door.

"No," Nate said. "We'll go out the back and swing around through the trees. We'll stay downwind that way."

When they got outside, Nate locked the door.

Brian watched, holding his rifle in both hands, pointing skyward. "Why are you locking the door?"

"I told you there's an egg thief sneaking around. We don't want him in the house, do we?"

"Is that what the military stuff is for?"

"I wouldn't shoot a hungry man for stealing eggs. Nothing else has been taken or damaged…yet. The trouble is—what will he do next? If I catch him, I'll try to hold him at gunpoint long enough to have a talk with him and let him know we'll give him what food we can spare if he would just ask first. And I will warn him not to come back sneaking around in the night 'cause he might get buckshot in him."

Brian smiled. "Oh."

They made their way through the trees. Nate took his time, keeping an eye out both for anything moving and tracks in the snow.

Brian followed a few yards behind, much less alert than his father but enjoying the late afternoon hike in the woods and a chance to be with his father on another hunt.

Nate stopped suddenly, looking to his left. Brian searched the woods for what his father was looking at. Then he saw smoke rising through the treetops in a stand of oaks and pines, drifting lazily in the still, cold air a half mile away near the top of a hill.

Brian eased up to his father. "Someone camping up there." He spoke not much louder than a whisper.

"That's what it looks like. Doesn't seem to be a wildfire. Just one thin column of smoke."

"Maybe it's the egg thief."

"Maybe. He's on federal land and not bothering us at the moment. Keep your eyes open. We'll go ahead and try to get that hog."

"He'll hear the shot."

"Yes he will. Might warn him not to steal from us anymore."

Brian sighed. "Sometimes I think you don't tell me everything."

"You know as much as I do about that smoke and the egg thief. Come on, let's get that porker. We need the meat."

"We could buy some hamburger in town."

"Come on now, and be quiet."

Nate led Brian to a thick stand of immature pines and found the oak windfall he was looking for. "Sit down behind this log and get comfortable."

Brian used a pine for a backrest. "Whoever is up there isn't too smart. I mean, he must know we can see that smoke. If I was stealing from somebody I would try to hide better."

"That's good thinking. But I know you wouldn't just try to hide, you would hide. I taught you better than that."

"If you think I'm so smart, why won't you tell me everything?"

"Like what?"

"Why don't we go into town anymore? We're not taking care of Beth or Mom, so there's no reason not to now."

"The sickness will be anywhere people are. Now let's stop talking. We need that meat, and talking is not the thing to do while hunting, you know that." He turned facing the house. His eyes scanned the woods in a wide arc, covering the area behind Brian. "Stay alert. If you see anything, man or animal, whisper."

"At least the sun will set behind us and to my left, out of our eyes," Brian said.

"I wonder how that happened."

"Oh come on. I'm not that stupid. You got us sitting downwind too."

"You're not stupid, period."

"But I was never in the Army and don't have your training."

"You have me. And I'm going to be teaching you a lot of things over the coming months. But you have to listen to me to learn. What did I say about talking while hunting?"

"That hog's not going to hear us whispering, Dad. You're making me think we're the ones being hunted."

"We know there's a thief in the area, and we know there's smoke up on that hill. I wouldn't say we're being hunted though. We have to be careful now. Things have gotten rough. There might not be much law anymore. Probably a lot of cops have died, leaving them shorthanded." He scanned the woods while talking. "Now be quiet so we can hear if something walks up."

"You mean a man."

"Quiet, I said."

The sun set behind the tree line and the air turned colder. They sat and searched the woods as all color faded to darkening gray. Brian pulled his collar up and stuffed his gloved hands back into his coat pocket. His father had told him years ago that sunup and sunset is the prime hunting time. He also knew from experience how cold you can get sitting at a deer stand. He had worn his heaviest coat, but he was still getting colder by the minute.

Nate tapped Brian on the shoulder. "Don't move and don't make a sound. Someone just ran behind the barn. He's got a rifle or shotgun. He's no egg thief."

Brian jerked his head towards the house.

"Don't move!" Nate hissed. "There's another one back in the trees to the right of the house."

"They mean to hurt us." Brian's breathing was fast and strong.

"Calm down. They don't know where we are. Breathe normal. You're puffing up a cloud of mist."

"What are we—?"

"Sshh. I'll handle it. I won't let anyone hurt you."

The sound of glass breaking just made it to Brian's young ears, but Nate did not hear it.

"They're breaking in," Brian said. "I thought you shuttered all the windows before we left."

"I see him."

The man pulled himself partway into the window. A loud boom shattered the peace of the cold twilight.

Brian gasped as he looked toward the house. A man lay in the snow under the window. He did not move.

Gunfire erupted from the woods. Like fireflies, muzzle flashes flickered in the dark of the forest. Someone was shooting at the house. Nate was already aiming. His left arm was in the shooting sling and he in a steady sitting position. He squeezed the trigger and saw the second man go down. Though it was dark in the shade of the trees, he knew his shot was a solid hit. If he was not dead, he would be soon.

He pushed Brian to the ground and against the oak windfall. "Crawl to the other end of the log and get behind that rock. Stay low. On your belly. Hurry!"

His eyes wide, Brian belly-crawled to the rock and sat behind it.

"No. On your belly. And stay there. Just lie there and don't move. I'll be back in an hour or so."

"An hour!"

"Shut up and do what I say. They're here to kill us."

Nate crawled twenty yards farther back into the forest and then rushed another twenty through thick brush while bent down low. His crashing could be heard by Brian or anyone else nearby, but silence was not important at the moment. His gunfire had given their position away, and he could only hope if someone was close enough to hear it would lead them away from Brian. He stopped and stood, taking advantage of the extra darkness under an oak tree in the gathering twilight and looked around, peering into the darkening woods. There was no sound, no movement.

His four years in the Army came back to him as if the decade and a half between then and now had been instantly removed with a surgeon's scalpel, seamlessly shortening his life. He was twenty-two again. A trained killer. A hunter of men. His wife had known something of his former life, but his children did not. He had always hoped they never would.

In the dark under the forest canopy, Nate found no one but the man he shot. He did not go to the house to check on the man who tried to crawl through Beth's bedroom window. He was dead. That was good enough for him. There was no need to expose himself in the open.

By the time Nate was able to slowly make his way around behind the farm all the way to the river, it was too dark to see anything, not even tracks in the snow. But there was no one out there. He was sure of that.

It took him another hour to make his way back around to Brian, gathering the dead man's weapons on the way.

"Brian." Nate's voice came out of the dark.

Brian jumped. "Jesus Christ, Dad!"

"Keep it low. I'm sure there's no one else around, but we can't be too careful. You only have one life, Son, value it. Don't give it away with carelessness."

"I was afraid I might shoot you thinking you were one of them."

"Good. That means you're thinking like a man and not a boy. I was hoping you were using your brain. Now I know you were." He put his hand on his son's head. He was not shaking from fear, but from cold. "You should have brought a hat with you." Nate was wearing a boonie hat. "It's okay now. Follow me. We'll skirt the tree line and stay in the shade. It's too dark to walk in the trees, and no one can see us on the other side of the field that way. Just stay close behind me and try to be as quiet as possible. I'll go slow, and we will come in through the trees behind the house and use the backdoor."

Brian got up from the ground and stood in the dark. "Is it safe to go to the house?"

"If there's any more shooting, jump into the woods and crawl behind cover and stay there until I come to get you."

"So you don't know if there's more." Brian looked around but could see little in the dark.

"I'm ninety-nine percent sure it's over. Just do what I say and it will be okay." Nate started walking.

Nate crawled to the backdoor and reached up with keys to open it. He swung it open and rolled out of the way. "Come on."

Brian broke from the tree line and ran all-out through the doorway and crashed into a chair before he could stop.

Nate closed the door and locked it. "You okay?"

"I think I flattened that chair you left by the hallway though. I can't see in here at all."

"We have plenty of chairs. I only have one son. Are you hurt?"

"No."

"Follow me."

They groped their way in the dark and into Beth's bedroom. It still smelled of her sickness, even with the window smashed and cold air entering. Nate removed the pump shotgun and unattached the wire to the trigger. He put the safety on and pumped a shell into the chamber. Reaching over to the dresser top, he groped in the dark, knocking over the buckshot shell he left there, just catching it before it rolled off onto the floor. He shoved it into the magazine.

"You set a shotgun in the window and didn't tell me?" Brian's voice rose in the dark. "And you knew there was trouble and said nothing. That's not right, Dad. You think I'm just a kid."

Nate shoved more rounds in the magazine. "I will do anything to protect you. It all worked out well."

"And you killed them like it was nothing. How do you know they were going to kill us?"

Nate's face hardened. "Goddamn it, think, Brian! And you say I should have told you? Things have changed. If you were older you would understand that." He put his heavy hand on Brian's shoulder. "I will kill anyone who tries to hurt you. And I make no apologies for it."

Nate looked out the window at the dead man. A circle of dried crimson surrounded his head, crusting in the snow. He closed and latched the shutters.

"Go to your room and get all the blankets you have and your sleeping bag. Take them to the bathroom and put them in the bathtub. Here. Keep this shotgun ready. That means in your hands."

"What?"

"Just do it. I'm going back out to get the man's guns."

Brian heard his father lock the front door when he came back in.

"Come on," Nate said. They slid along the hallway wall in the dark and entered Beth's bedroom. Nate unloaded the dead man's guns, letting the cartridges fall on the bed, and then laid them on the mattress with the actions open. "Stay here," he said. He came back with the rifle and pistol he took off the man in the woods and unloaded them and put them on the mattress beside the others. "Got that shotgun in your hands?"

"Yes." Brian's voice sounded unsure.

"Good. Follow me."

When they were in the bathroom, Nate asked, "Where's your rifle?"

"Leaning against the wall between the sink and the toilet."

"Good. Is it loaded?"

"I…I thought you wanted me to leave it loaded tonight."

"You thought right. From now on all of our guns are loaded except when we're cleaning them. Understand?"

"Yes." Brian nodded, his chest pumping fast.

"I know this is all scary, but calm down," Nate said. "I taught you to treat all guns as if they are loaded whether they are or not. That means never point it at anyone you do not want to kill."

"I know. Now that we are keeping them loaded all the time it's even more important."

"And," Nate said, "we're going to be jumpy with the danger of people showing up to hurt us, so we've got to be alert and careful at all times. We don't want to shoot each other by accident." He spread Brian's sleeping bag in the bottom of the tub, covering the end opposite the fixtures and all the bottom. "Give me the shotgun." Brian did as directed. "Now wrap yourself in the blankets. And sit down in the tub."

"Why all this?"

"I will be a while, probably near to daylight, burying the one in the woods and dragging the one by the window to the river. Hopefully the current will take him downstream and the gators will eat him. If there are any gators left that haven't froze to death. We don't need to be smelling him."

"Can't we bury him too?" Brian sat in the tub.

Nate handed Brian his shotgun. "We're both going to be up all night as it is. Burying people is not what's going to keep us alive."

"Okay. I'll stay here with the shotgun."

"That's the idea," Nate said. "When I come back, I will speak out so you can recognize my voice. If anyone comes through that door that does not sound like me or says nothing, shoot—and keep shooting as long as there is anything still breathing. If you run the shotgun dry, grab your rifle and keep shooting. Remember, both will shoot through these walls and kill anyone behind them."

"Okay. Just don't forget to speak out."

"I won't, Brian." He laughed. "I promise you that."

Chapter 3

Morning came and Nate was still up, watching and listening. Brian was asleep in bed, dead tired.

Nate waited until ten before firing up the stove and cooking some canned corned beef and potatoes. He was not going out to the chicken coop for eggs until he had a better look around in daylight. It would do for breakfast. He wished he had some ketchup for Brian. At least there was still bread and coffee.

Nate turned on the shortwave and punched buttons until he got two hams talking about the violence in their area: Orlando. "There ain't a single deputy on duty in this county," a man with a gravelly voice said. "And the city cops disappeared weeks ago. Probably most are dead. The few that aren't are protecting their own families."

Nate yelled down the hallway. "Brian. Time to wake up and eat. And there's something on the radio I want you to hear."

Waking with a start in his bed, eyes wide open and fully alert, Brian asked, "What's wrong?"

"Time to eat. Everything's okay." Nate turned the radio up.

"Most of downtown is burned to the ground, the stores all looted, picked clean," the second voice said his voice revealing fear and dismay. "And what they're taking is insane. How in the hell is a TV or computer going to keep you alive? You can't eat them. And there's no power anyway."

"What's that he's saying, Dad?" Brian yelled from down the hall.

"Listen while you eat." Nate set another plate on the table.

Brian stood in his socks and the clothes he wore the night before, rubbing his eyes and yawning. "This is the first time you let me listen to the radio in months. Since the power went out. You said it would run the battery down and there was nothing on it anyway." His eyes lit up. "What about the TV?"

"The solar panel has recharged the batteries by now, but the TV will use too much power. None of the stations are on anyway. They have no power either. This isn't a commercial station, it's ham radio, shortwave. People are talking to one another like the cops on their car radios. Just listen and learn about what's going on now that the sickness has taken most people in America, probably the world."

As they ate, more ham radio operators joined the conversation. It was getting too bleak and descriptive, so Nate checked other stations until a commercial shortwave station out of London came in.

A woman's voice in British accent came from the speaker. "As we have been saying all along, please stay indoors and off the streets. There is nothing to be done for your loved ones. Most hospitals are shut down for lack of personnel and power. There are no medications for this disease, so you must stay home and care for your loved ones there. Just keep them in bed and as comfortable as possible until the end." A man broke in. "And please be careful with candles and fire. It's overcast and cold tonight, but you must be careful trying to stay warm with fire. Many fires are burning throughout London at this moment, and there is no way to fight them. There are not enough healthy personnel left to provide any municipal services at all. You are on your own. This may be the last night we broadcast. The generator is running low on petrol. God be with you."

"Is it like that everywhere?" Brian asked.

Nate turned the radio off. "The last I heard, the sickness was all over the globe."

Brian swallowed hard and looked inward. "We can't go to town, can we?"

"No." Nate's eyes locked on his son.

"People are killing each other 'cause they're scared and hungry and cold."

"Yes."

"I don't blame you for killing those men. You couldn't just call the sheriff."

"It's just us, Brian. Our nearest neighbors are all dead. Except maybe Mel. Being in the Guard, he was called to duty early on. I didn't say anything to you at the time. Maybe he's alive, maybe not. Anyway, we've got to take care of each other and get by with what we have here."

Brian smiled, all sign of worry leaving his face. "Ha! Mel, he's a real nut. Always talking about surviving the end of the world as we know it. Remember that song he always listened to? All those guns and ammo he kept!"

"I'm thinking he wasn't such a nut after all." Nate put his fork down. "Before he left, he asked me to keep an eye on his place and said if we needed anything to help ourselves to his cache of food. He knew how bad it had already gotten and was afraid he might not make it back."

"That was six months ago. I hope he does come back. He was always good to us, even if he was a survivalist nut."

"I wish he were here now," Nate said. "We could use another…hand in the field come spring."

"There you go again, Dad. What you meant was we need another man who can fight in case more men come to kill us. I'm not a kid anymore. You should stop hiding things from me like you did Beth."

"Eat," Nate said. "Your food is getting cold. We need him for a lot of things. We could band with our other neighbors too…if they had lived. His place is a lot more defendable than our farm. I'm thinking about moving into that bunker of his and waiting it out. In a few more months the population will thin out even more and there will be fewer men able to walk out here to bother us. Starving people can't walk far, and we're thirty-five miles out in farm country. Gas is running out, so they can't drive out here much longer. The dirt roads aren't being maintained. Come summer and heavy rain, maybe a hurricane, they will be washed out. I hope anyway."

Brian stopped eating and just sat and looked at his father.

"I'm the same man I was before, Brian. It's the world that's changed, not me. I did not do this to the world anymore than I killed your mother and sister. The world is out of our hands. We're going to have a hard enough time just taking care of each other." He looked at Brian across the table. "Like we did last night. I'm proud of you. But I always was."

Brian looked down at his food. "We can't help anyone?"

"If someone we knew we could trust showed up, it would be a help to us."

Brian looked across the table at his father. "You mean if it was Mel, someone who could help us survive."

"Anyone we could trust. With just the two of us, it's going to be hard to keep a twenty-four-hour watch. We must set up security procedures and two people just isn't enough. We have to sleep. And someone has to watch for trouble while the other takes care of the animals and does all the other work around here. We can't be careless like we've been. That's over. It's too dangerous now. People are starving and there is no law."

"It's scary."

"Yes it is."

Brian cocked his head, his face showing puzzlement. "I just remembered the fire last night. Up on the hill. Did you ever check it?"

Nate drank from a glass of water. "I didn't have time. I think that fire was a ruse to lure us up there and into an ambush. When we didn't take the bait, they came down after us." He stood. "I'm going to check out the area, including the hill. Stay inside. Keep the doors and shutters locked and that shotgun within arm's reach at all times."

"Okay. But how did you know they were around even before you saw the smoke? The egg thief?"

"They were not after eggs. Someone else is the egg thief. It was the egg thief who woke me up and made me more aware of things though. When you've been hunted…something happens inside you. You learn to sense danger…when you're being hunted…I just knew."

"I wish I could learn that."

"I hope you never do. I hope last night is the closest you ever come to…"

"You're scared for me, more than anything else."

"Yes. Just do what I tell you and we should be okay."

"I'm trying."

"I know. I better go. It will be late when I get back. I want to swing around wide and check things out around the area and go over to Mel's place too. So don't worry unless I'm not back by late tonight."

"Okay. But try to be back before it's too dark. The cow has to be milked and fed, and I want to churn some butter, we're out."

Nate's face softened. "Remember; don't go outside until I get back. I can milk the cow tonight if need be. She's not producing much now since we can't let her out to graze. The cow will be okay until tonight. Why don't you grind some wheat and bake a couple loaves? We're out of bread too."

Brian glanced at the wood box and saw there was plenty of firewood. "What about the smoke?"

"You're thinking, keep doing that. I'll be around for the most part, up in the hills and watching. If there are more men around, the smoke may make them think we're both inside. I can hear your gunfire from a mile away. One shot and I will come running and pick them off if they sneak up to the house. There will be a time when I can't see, when I'm at Mel's place. But otherwise I will be watching. Just stay in the house. "

"Oh."

"See you late this evening. And put that steel bar across the door after I'm out."

*   *   *

Nate flowed through the woods at man-hunting speed, staying in the shadows and choosing his path with cover and concealment in mind, the Ranger way. He did not think anyone was around. The two he killed was all of them. There was the egg thief, but so far this person had done them no harm. Probably just a hungry refugee from town, he thought.

Fresh snow covered the men's tracks, but he could tell the fire had been built and then quickly abandoned. Certainly it was a ruse to lure them up the hill and into an ambush.

On the way to Mel's property, Nate found a fresh kill. Someone had snared a rabbit and skinned and gutted it sometime around daylight. Snow had not covered the tracks, and despite the heavy boots, it was obvious this person was not large. Since the trail was going his way, he followed cautiously, staying off to the side and in cover. A mile and a half from Mel's place, the tracks led into a stand of small pines that were growing thick, offering good concealment for anyone wanting to hide. He eased into the maze but stopped after one hundred yards. He was coming into rough country, with a multitude of ambush sites. Too dangerous to go on just to satisfy his curiosity, he turned and headed for Mel's bunker.

If he did not know where it was, he might never find it. Surrounded by national forest land, and with no roads leading to it, Mel had picked a good location for a survivalist retreat.

Nate searched out a route that a cow could travel while keeping in cover. His plan was to transport all the livestock to Mel's place and keep them hid as well as possible. But that would have to wait for warmer weather and would require Brian and him to raise enough hay for the cow on their farm next summer while maintaining security. That would not be easy. Working in an open field is a good way to get shot if any more hungry people came around. They also had to carry enough chicken feed on their backs through rough, hilly country; enough to last a year. It would take many trips. Anything they left behind would most likely be looted. The home and barn could even be burned to the ground.

Moving slowly through the woods, enjoying the warmth of the sun and being outdoors, his mind raced back to happier days when he was a boy. He grew up on the farm he now owned, and, as a boy, spent nearly every spare hour away from school and farm work walking these woods, hunting, fishing, trapping, and camping. In those days the only worries he had was making certain he did not raise the ire of his father. Then came the Army, and for a solid year, and then another, life-and-death decisions came every day in a hot, cold, dry, sandy, hellhole. One mistake and those he served with, innocent civilians who got in the way, not to mention him, would die. He remembered the Ranger RT leader who called in a fire mission on top of his own men. Five died in a second. One mistake and five good men died. The RT leader committed suicide three days later. And there was South America. This one a jungle war.

Then came marriage and a son and daughter. More responsibilities. With those responsibilities came the most satisfying part of his life. Now, he had only his son, and all the care and love he had for his wife and daughter was concentrated and focused on Brian. The plague left him with one goal: to give Brian a chance to live through the years ahead. He must give Brian a chance to have a life. The coming years would be hell. But the human race would fight up out of the dirt, dust itself off, and rebuild. He intended to make certain Brian lived long enough to see the rebuilding and enjoy the better times that surely will come. Someday. Someday.

Nate went to Mel's bunker first. From a distance of only fifty yards, it appeared to be nothing more than a grassy mound. A few pine seedlings grew on the sod-covered concrete roof. Protruding from the roof were ventilation pipes, but you could not see them through the grass and weeds growing on the dirt that covered the whole bunker. The heavy steel door, painted olive drab for camouflage, had an overelaborate set of bolts of two inch thick steel rods (two hidden and nearly impossible to find unless you knew their exact location), locks, and latches. Only high explosives or a bulldozer could force it. The padlock was just the beginning of many obstacles to getting the door open. Nate noticed that no one had bothered it.

The door was protected by a concrete wall five feet high; some four feet back from the door. It was bermed too, with grass-covered dirt. Between the door and the wall was a perfect place to shoot from in relative safety. It did force anyone wanting to enter the bunker to come in from a right angle, but that was a small price to pay for the extra security it offered.

On all four sides, just above where the berms ended, ventilation and shooting slots were shuttered from inside with heavy steel plating. They were not visible behind the winter-killed grass that had grown tall on the berms now that Mel was not there to cut it.

There was no need to go inside. No one had bothered the door. More than likely, no one had been in the area since Mel left.

Nate went on to the cave. It was Mel's cache, full of years' worth of food and other survival supplies. The entranceway was well-hidden and equipped with the same massive door and hidden bolts as the bunker. It would make for an even safer place to hide, but there was no ventilation and anyone inside would die of lack of oxygen unless the door was left open. Also, there was no water supply. The bunker had a well and hand pump inside. There was also a toilet that flushed into a septic tank buried deep and off to the side of the bunker. You had to fill a bucket with the pump and then use the water to flush with. A small number of people could stay in that bunker for a long time without ever coming out.

It took him several minutes to unlock the large hacksaw and bolt cutter resistant locks with two different keys Mel had given him, and pull the hidden bolts. They went through four feet of rock and into holes in heavy steal brackets on the inside of the door. Mel had to rent a special drill to bore the long holes. A bush covered the holes where the bolts came out of the rock, ending with a Tee-handle.

Nate smiled as he pulled the heavy door open. "Thank God for crazy survivalists. You're not crazy if the sky actually is falling."

He walked inside and stood long enough for his eyes to adjust to the dark. It was warmer in the cave. Unlike most caves in Florida, this one was relatively dry with less humidity in the air captured inside with the door closed. Sixty-five feet long and twenty wide, the cavern was filled to its ten foot ceiling with plastic forty-five gallon boxes and five gallon buckets with sealed covers. There were also many barrels of ten gallon to fifty-five gallon size, most were plastic. Every container was labeled: wheat; rice; freeze-dried beef stew…

Far in the back, behind boxes labeled "FD lasagna w/meat," he found one marked: "condiments." He stuffed a one-gallon can of freeze-dried ketchup in his backpack and then a can of lasagna. It took moving boxes aside to find the powdered drink mix. There was just enough room in his pack for a quart-sized can each of powdered orange drink and chocolate mix. All of the items were for Brian.

After securing the cave door back as he found it, Nate walked a wide circle around the area, looking for sign of anyone having been on Mel's land. The only thing he found was a snare set for rabbits. Snow had covered any tracks. Part of him wanted to stay and wait for the owner to check the snare. But he needed to get back to Brian. Whoever it was had done him no harm. Perhaps he had stolen a few eggs, if it was the same person, but even if it was, he had no quarrel with him. Nate stayed on high alert all the way back to the farm.

*   *   *

"I picked up a few things at Mel's cache." Nate pulled the cans out of his pack and set them on the kitchen counter.

Brian rolled his eyes. "Ketchup. So you think I was going to die without it?"

"Well, now, aren't you the appreciative one. It's not like you have to eat it. The can's not opened yet, and it can stay that way."

"It will sure make the eggs taste better."

"Especially when you burn them."

"Now you're picking on me."

"You deserve to be picked on. You haven't said thank you yet. I carried this stuff many miles." He lifted the two smaller cans out of the pack. "Either of these will go with breakfast too."

Brian's eyes flickered with light. He tried to appear blasé.

"And this will provide a few dinners." Nate set the can of lasagna down.

Brian smiled and said, "That's okay, but couldn't you have brought more stuff while you were there?"

He tried to run but Nate caught him by the neck. "Okay smart-mouth, you cook tonight while I milk and feed the cow. After we eat, you churn butter."

"Cook? All you do is heat water and put in the freeze-dried stuff and stir a little."

"You're right." Nate saw plates and cups piled by the sink. "That means you can do the dishes too."

"Should we say a prayer for Mel tonight?" Brian had a mischievous smile on his face.

"You're still being a smartass," Nate said. "You pray? We should certainly have him own our minds as we enjoy his food, that's for sure."

"We can tell each other Mel-stories while we eat."

Nate gave Brian a fake dirty look. "You know, I hope he comes home someday so I can tell him how you've been talking about him while he was gone. And while you eat his food too."

Brian waved him off. "He won't care."

Chapter 4

"What is this about?" Brian asked. They were in the barn and Nate was fabricating a wood frame twelve inches square.

Nate hammered the last nail in. It was ready for the hardware cloth. He had put a door on it with a simple latch to keep animals out and a roof cut from a sheet of tin roofing material to shed rain and snow. "I hope we don't get a smart coon up here from the river swamp that learns how to open this."

"What is it for?" Brian looked Nate's project over.

"We're going to put a few eggs in it at night. I will nail it to the wall outside the coop."

"Why? They will probably freeze."

"If they're still here in the morning we will eat them for breakfast." Nate grabbed wire cutters.

"You're baiting the egg thief so you can catch him? What are you going to do if you do catch him?"

"No." Nate shook his head. He was disappointed in Brian. "I'm giving him the eggs. Whoever it is has been living on rabbits. A person can die of starvation with a stomach full of rabbit meat in him. I found snares when I went to Mel's. And a place where he skinned and gutted one. There's not enough fat in rabbit meat. Especially in the winter. And this has been a bad one, even worse than last year."

"Yeah, I remember you told me you can't live on rabbit alone." Brian seemed puzzled, but he said nothing more.

"Why don't you paint up a sign? Make it black letters on white and large enough to see on a moonlit night."

"What? We shoot egg thieves?" Brian had a smirk on his face.

"How about free eggs?" Nate could see he was joking. "Afterwards we'll go hog hunting—for real this time. We need some fresh meat."

"And we can't buy it in town," Brian added.

An hour later, they were both through with their projects.

"It won't be dry enough to paint the letters until tomorrow," Brian said.

"Good work."

"I just painted it white. The hard part is painting the words."

"Clean the brush?"

"Yep."

Nate pointed to the paint on Brian's hands. "Clean yourself up. Then we'll eat and go hunting."

"The hog will smell the turpentine on my hands."

"That's good thinking. The paint smell is on both of us. We'll stay downwind. Hogs are not as hard to hunt as whitetails. Wash your hands good with dish detergent to get the turpentine off. It's not good for you to have it on your skin anyway."

"There wasn't any water-based paint." Brian looked at his painted hands.

"I know. I'll pump the water for you. Wash your hands quick when we get out there. We will be in the open."

Brian looked up at his father, his easy smile gone. "No one's been around since those two."

"You never can tell. But I don't think there's anyone around."

After lunch, they headed into the woods. Brian had his Marlin 30/30 and Nate the M14. He wore his load-bearing harness with six extra 20 round magazines. Both wore olive drab boonie hats and green coats and they carried military surplus ALICE packs to bring the meat back to the farm.

Nate kept them in heavy cover and swung around to the river a mile downstream. Unlike their farm, the land along the river downstream was low and swampy. The river valley on both sides flooded after heavy summer rain and was populated with wild hogs: the offspring of feral pigs escaped from other farms.

They slowly worked their way around muddy spots, many rooted up by hogs looking for grubs and other things only a hog would eat. The swamp smell was not strong like in the heat of summer, but down in the river valley the humidity was higher. And under the shade of the canopy of treetops, it was colder. Finding nothing but tracks and rooted areas as large as a half acre, Nate decided to go back up on drier ground and into a large stand of oak trees. He whispered to Brian, "It's too cold for them to be down here in the wet. They're eating acorns and staying out in the sun."

Brian nodded.

"We'll come in quiet and get between them and their usual retreat route to safety. Go slow and stay back about five yards." Nate followed a hog trail that had been cut up with fresh tracks.

Just where swamp turned into upland and the trees turned from cypress and hickory to magnolia, Nate spotted a small pine that had been scarred by the tusks of a boar. There was a circle of torn ground where the boar had repeatedly slashed the tree, creating a doughnut of raw earth with the pine in the middle as he worked his way around the trunk. The marks on the pine and tracks in the dirt were fresh. A few minutes later they found trees smeared with wet mud and others with mud dried over several days where a hog had rubbed its sides, leaving mud high enough to reach Nate's belt buckle.

Nate motioned for Brian to come to him and pointed at a muddy tree. He whispered, "We don't want that one. He's a big boar. He'll be tough and gamy."

"And he's a mean SOB," Brian added.

Nate smiled slightly at his language and walked on. As they worked their way up on higher ground, Nate kept them downwind of the stand of oaks he wanted to hunt.

Brian tapped him on the shoulder. He stopped.

"I hear one up there to the left," Brian said.

Nate nodded, though he had heard nothing but the occasional rustling of brush in the slight breeze and their own footsteps in the mud earlier and now the crunch of dry leaves underfoot. "We will have to slow more to be quiet. Keep your eyes and ears open."

They were forced to go through a thick patch of saw palmetto before they could get to the oaks. Nate searched for a route through which they could penetrate without alerting every animal in the area. He found a place that looked somewhat easier to get through and slowly slipped between the chest-high, wide, green fronds. Two thirds of the way though, a boar grunted and a sow squealed.

Two sows came running toward the patch of saw palmetto and turned to face some unknown danger in a small clearing just ten yards from Nate. One of the sows had piglets. They scurried under and around her, obviously as excited as the sows. A three-hundred-pound boar rushed into the clearing, its bristles straight up on its back, and turned to face something in the brush on the far side, popping its jaws, tusks slashing. Another hog squealed as if it were in the jaws of death further back in the woods. The boar in the clearing was bleeding from both shoulders and one side of its head.

A rumbling noise like that of a two-cycle engine on a chainsaw that had just been revved up and now was coasting down in revolutions per minute came from the direction the hogs were looking. Something large crashed through the brush, coming closer at a fast rate.

Nate knew what it was and was sure Brian did too. He had intended to let Brian harvest the meat on this trip, mainly for training and target practice. Brian might be killing another kind of animal soon. Not for meat, but self-defense. But Brian was to his left and slightly behind. He was not in position to shoot because Nate was in the way, and there was no time for him to maneuver around him.

Nate brought his rifle up and shouldered it in one motion. He fired once. The sow with no piglets rolled over, got up and tried to run, squealing its head off. Then its legs collapsed under it, and it fell on its belly and died.

The other sow took off squealing. Its piglets ran in every direction squealing for all they were worth. The boar in the clearing stretched out its massive body, and in three long, jumping strides, disappeared into the brush on Nate's right. Nate and Brian both tracked its rapid progress with their ears as it crashed like a bull through heavy saw palmettos. It swung around behind them and headed for the river. The last they heard of it was splashing as it raced through a wet area down in the swamp.

Nate turned to Brian and said, "Well, let's get this one—"

Another boar came bulldozing its way into the clearing and made for Nate at full speed, popping its mouth and slashing with four inch tusks, rumbling like a motorcycle, stiff back bristles standing straight up. It was half again as large as the boar that ran into the swamp.

Brian thumbed back his rifle's hammer, threw down on him and fired in one quick motion. He was off to the side a little and had to aim for the right shoulder. The massive boar's front right quarter collapsed and the animal slid on dry leaves carpeting the ground. It struggled to right itself. Brian worked the lever, keeping the Marlin on his shoulder the way Nate had taught him, and shot into the animal's brain, killing it instantly.

Nate had the boar in his sights but never fired. He lowered the M14 and turned to Brian. "Damn good shooting, Son."

Brian looked across the clearing at the dead boar, his face stoic. "You're the one who taught me and put the peep sight on with the big aperture for snap shooting in thick cover."

Nate appraised his son. Nodding, he said, "You're coming along just fine, Brian. Just fine." His chest rose and he let out a sigh. "We will be up most of the night butchering and hauling meat. That old boar's going to be sausage. Otherwise it'll be like chewing on these old boots I'm wearing."

"At least it will be plenty cold and the meat won't spoil."

"Yeah. I was hoping for warmer weather, but now I hope it stays cold for a few days longer anyway."

"We can smoke some of the sow," Brian said.

"And can some of the boar. You can't tell one meat from another once it's been cooked to death for canning, and it tenderizes the toughest meat. I think we should leave a ham off that old boar for the egg thief too."

"We will have to hang it some way to keep the rats and other animals off it," Brian said. "It sure won't fit in that little wire box you made for the eggs."

"Yep, that's true. Let's get busy."

Before starting the messy job at hand, they stood by the massive boar, taking in its size.

Brian pulled his five inch sheath knife. "You think the egg thief will want these mountain oysters?"

Nate laughed. "Maybe. Unless you want them."

"No thanks."

Brian bent down and checked the long tusks. "He could have done some damage with those." He looked up while testing the sharp edges with his index finger. "This has to be the biggest one you've ever seen. A wild one I mean."

"No. Your grandfather killed one larger back before I went into the Army. This one's a close second."

Brian looked disappointed. "And I thought I might have impressed you by killing the biggest boar you ever saw."

"Oh, you impressed me all right: with your shooting." Nate took his coat off and put it on the ground out of the way. "Lift his hind leg up and I'll gut him." He spoke as he rolled up his shirtsleeves.

Nate slit him open quickly and pulled out the warm entrails.

"Okay, let's get the sow open and bled."

"I can do that one," Brian said.

"Next time. My arms are already soaked in this stinking blood. Notice how hog blood and guts stink a lot more than deer?"

Brian nodded. "It's a whole different smell, much worse."

"I'll get it this time, we're in a hurry."

When Nate had two of the legs partially skinned on the sow, he stood up and walked around to the back of the animal. "I'll pull while you cut the hide loose in the tough spots."

Soon, they had it skinned back to the spine. Nate started quartering it. They put two of the quarters in plastic garbage bags.

Nate picked up a quarter. "Bring my pack over and hold it open."

Brian held the pack while Nate slid the hindquarter in.

"I think I can get this front quarter in too." Nate rolled the sow over and had the front leg and quarter skinned, off, and in the pack in less than five minutes.

"Dad, don't lie, you've done this before, haven't you?"

Nate laughed. "Once or twice. You were there the last few times."

"But you let me do more of the work."

"We're pressed for time." He began to skin the last hindquarter. "I'll pull, you cut. Just like before. In about ten minutes we'll be starting on the boar."

It was nearly dark by the time they had a front quarter from the sow in Brian's pack and the boar skinned and quartered. They hung the spine and ribs of both sow and boar and the quarters of the boar from ropes tied to tree limbs.

"That's high enough only a bear could reach it," Nate said. "Let's get the last quarter from the sow hung."

"Bears and coyotes will be after the guts over there first anyway." Brian wiped his hands on his pants.

"Yep. That's why we hung the meat over here. They'll smell the guts first and eat that. We're going to make one more trip tonight anyway."

"Won't be able to get it all though," Brian said. "That boar is humungous. And it's not even really fat. It's all muscle."

Nate stretched his aching back. "I'm thinking we'll bring what we don't get to the farm over to that large pine with the limb hanging out straight. The one that's almost to our field. We can hang it there and it'll be safe till morning."

"You think a bear will find it tonight?"

"If there's one within a mile of here, it will damn sure smell those guts. They have a nose on them. And he'll eat it all, including the contents of the stomach and intestines."

"Oh shit!" Brian made a face like he was going to gag.

"Get my canteen and pour water on my hands and arms so I can wash some of this sticky blood off before we start for home."

*   *   *

"Dad, I'm beat." Brian looked up at the pork hanging from rafters in their barn.

"You should be," Nate said. "We got it all done though, and it's only midnight. Now we need to clean up and eat. I'll let you sleep late while I get the rest of the boar in the morning."

"No. Wake me. You need my help."

Nate looked at his son—and said nothing.

"What?"

"You know if you hadn't shot that big ass boar, we would have been done hours ago." His face was unreadable.

Brian was incredulous. "It was coming at you with those tusks!"

Nate shrugged his shoulders. "I could have shot it if I was afraid. It was feinting."

"It fainted all right. After I shot it in the head."

"Feint. Not faint."

"What?"

Nate swung at Brian's stomach. When he flinched and jumped to the side, Nate jabbed, tapping him on the forehead with an open hand. "I just feinted punching you in the stomach. When you reacted, I took advantage of the opening you left me and punched you in the face, or I could have. That's what feinting is." He looked at Brian, his face unreadable again. "Funny how you thought I was going to hit you for no reason. How many times have I ever done that?"

"Never. It was a reflex."

"That's why it worked so well. Actually, it was different with the boar. He may have been pretending to charge to bluff us out of his territory. On the other hand, he might have been serious. They have been known to slash people up. And this one was already riled. He had been fighting with the smaller boar and had attacked another hog back in the brush."

"I told you he was a mean SOB. Like some people. And big as a house. I never saw one that big."

"Yeah, I remember that. You're getting good at reading tracks."

"It was the tree he tore up, Dad." Brian rolled his eyes.

Nate laughed. "All right. Let's clean up and eat.

The next morning the ham they left hanging in front of the barn was gone. The eggs were untouched.

Brian pointed. "Look. He dragged it into the woods over there."

"Yeah. It was too heavy for him to carry in one piece. I bet he took it a ways into the woods and then cut it up so he could carry the pieces, making more than one trip. Whoever it is, is not very large. I could tell that by the tracks back when I found that rabbit snare."

"You think we should trail him?" Brian asked. "I mean so we can tell him we'll give what food we can spare as long as he means us no harm."

Nate thought for a moment. "Maybe after we've gotten the rest of the meat back here. Remember, we've got to smoke some, can some, and turn some into sausage. Right now, I want to fry some with our eggs. I'm hungry."

"Can't we freeze some?"

Nate examined a footprint as he talked. "We have only so much kerosene for the fridge, and we should save it for the hot months. In some ways, this winter's unusual cold is a blessing. We've had enough ice to keep butter and milk in the icebox at least."

Twenty minutes later, Brian sat at the table and chewed his ham slowly. "You sure this was the sow and not the boar?"

Nate chuckled. "It's the sow. Something wrong?"

"Gamy and tough."

"A little gamy, but I wouldn't call it tough. Next time we'll shoot a buck."

Brian stopped chewing. "This doesn't seem so bad after all."

"You're right," Nate said. "It's not bad at all. How about the eggs? You notice something different about them this morning?"

Brian kept his face unreadable. "You cooked them."

"And?"

"They're not burned." Brian swallowed, trying not to laugh.

"And where did the ketchup come from?" Nate leaned into the table, holding his ear closer as if he were trying to hear.

Brian rolled his eyes. "I'll remember to thank Mel…if he comes back. And I hope he does."

"Nice of you to be so grateful when people do things for you."

"Yep, I certainly will thank Mel if he comes back."

"All right smart aleck, finish up. We have another long day ahead of us."

Brian took two more bites of scrambled egg and a sip of coffee. "I'm done."

"Good. Get your pack."

*   *   *

"Bear!" Brian watched a black bear run into thick brush.

"It got one of the hams." Nate checked the meat, still hanging from the pine tree. "He didn't have time to get to the rest."

"I don't know if I should be angry or thankful. That boar is not really fit to eat, judging by what the sow tastes like."

Nate's expression revealed disappointment in Brian. "If you were the egg thief you wouldn't be so choosy. People are starving."

"But we have Mel's stuff."

"That won't last forever. We must stretch it out as much as possible. Also, it's not ours, even if he did say we could use it. Imagine if he comes back, thinking if he can just get back home he'll be okay and have food waiting for him, and he learns we have used it all."

Brian stood frozen, looking inward, his face showing shock. "You mean this could be forever? It won't get better and return to normal?"

"Oh hell. Brian, it will get better as people rebuild. But it will never be like it was exactly, not in our lifetime. From what I've heard on the radio, including early on, when the governments were still putting out information, at least ninety percent of the world's population has been killed by the sickness."

"We will never be able to go into town and buy food again? Never have power? Never have school or football or TV or computers or gas for the truck?"

"Most of those things will come back in time." The tone of Nate's voice was not reassuring.

"How long?" A look of disillusionment scurried across Brian's face. "I'm not going to eat wild hog and deer the rest of my life."

"You know it's not like that." Nate stepped closer. "We have years' worth of food at Mel's, and we will have fresh vegetables again in a few months when we get to work in the field. We'll have chicken when the hatchlings come in the spring and we stop eating all the eggs."

"We shouldn't be giving eggs to that damn thief if we don't have enough for ourselves." Brian looked at his father, anger on his face. "You don't tell me a damn thing."

Nate stepped closer. "Watch how you talk to me. I know you're hurting from the loss of your mother and sister, but striking out at me is wrong. You're pushing it. I didn't think you could handle it, and you are proving me right."

"What do I have to live for, really? How am I going to have any kind of a life now? Am I supposed to just stay here on this farm forever and never have a life?" Brian turned and looked into the woods. "I wanted to go to college and join the Air Force and fly jetfighters and become an astronaut."

"Many of those dreams would have been left behind as you matured anyway. And many things you want out of life are still there waiting for you. There's a government of some kind still...and a military. The schools will open again someday, maybe in a year or two—and the colleges. NASA will be restarted too." Nate's face hardened. "Now suck it up and stand straight and tall like you've been doing lately. You're fast becoming a man, and I am proud to be your father. Especially lately."

Brian spun on his heels to face his father. "If you think I'm so great, why do you keep lying to me?"

"There have been no lies. I have been telling you more as...time allowed. I've been busy you know. Taking care of your mother and then your sister. Yes, it's bad, but it's not as bad as you're making it out to be. The worst thing is the loss of your mother and sister. If you can handle that, you can take the rest. Now show me you're the kind of man I thought. Life is what it is, Brian. It's up to you to make the best of it. We have it easy compared to many. Imagine what it's like in town or a big city. The chaos and violence. The stench of millions of rotting bodies. My grandfather—your great-grandfather—grew up in the Depression in total poverty and then fought for years in World War II. He was wounded twice. Then he was sent back and died in Europe." He gave Brian a stern look. "So stop whining. And stop striking out at me because you are in pain. I'm going through it too, so stop it."

"I'm sorry." Brian looked away.

Nate kept quiet while he concentrated on holding his temper. He did not know if he should put a stop to Brian's backtalk or if he should go easy on him. He remembered a little of what it was like to be Brian's age, but his world did not collapse around him when he was a boy, and he did not lose half of his family in the span of only a few weeks. Brian's mood swings worried him a lot more than the backtalk. Nate knew Brian respected him. His episodes of belligerent verbal assaults started not long after the death of his mother. Perhaps the verbal outbursts were relieving emotional pressure. If so, the worst thing he could do was make Brian afraid of him by using violent punishment at a time when his son feared the future. He wanted Brian to feel safe with him and know he could talk to him whenever he needed. Nate had seen grown men snap under the kind of pressure Brian was under. He knew soldiers who committed suicide.

Nate took several more breathes before speaking. "Feeling sorry for ourselves is silly. We have this farm and Mel's supplies. Things aren't so bad here."

Brian looked up at him. "Yeah, we're having *so* much fun. I should be happy."

"Fun is a child's word. You're not a child anymore. Now let's get this meat to the house. We need it. There are starving men who would kill for one ounce of it."

Brian was silent as he helped Nate load the meat in their packs and then set off for home.

They said little on the second trip for more meat. Brian kept looking into the distance at nothing as he walked. Nate overloaded himself with a quarter and the spareribs. It was the last piece and he did not want to make an extra trip. Two thirds of the way home, he was forced to lighten his load and leave the spareribs hanging in a tree.

"I'm glad you did that, Dad," Brian said. "You had to bend over to carry it all. The ham alone must weight one hundred pounds. With the ribs and some of the pork loin tied on the back, it was too much."

He's back to normal again, after being in his own world while we work. He spent the time thinking. Probably sorry for what he said, but does not want to bring it up. "Well, now I have to make another trip. More of the day will be used up, and we won't have time to process much of the meat."

"I will can some while you're gone."

"No. You grind sausage. Just use the tool to push it in and keep your fingers out of the grinder and be careful with the knife. Canning is an all-day job, especially with a wood stove."

"Yeah, I know: you're afraid I'll blow myself up. Or burn myself."

"Water in that pressure cooker is certainly hot and dangerous. But it takes hours to do much canning and there is tomorrow for that. We're both going to be worn out when we hit the sack tonight as it is."

"What'll we use all that canned pork for anyway?" Brian's attitude became more cooperative.

"It can be used like any other canned meat. It can be put in stews, fried, even though it's already cooked, whatever."

"At least it won't be so tough anymore."

"Yep," Nate said. "You can't tell one meat from another once it's been canned. Though you will know it's not beef. You know: you've had canned venison."

"Venison burger's not bad. The canned stuff is okay in soup…if you're starving."

"Some people are. We can't waste anything. And remember, there is no hospital to go get sewed up or broken bones set. Be very careful about preventing injuries. A small thing can turn into something serious."

"I know, I know." Brian rolled his eyes.

"Talk like that makes me wonder if you do."

Chapter 5

The sun was not up yet, and it was fifteen degrees. It had snowed again, covering the ground with Florida sugar two inches deep. Nate walked into the house, holding a pail of eggs. "It is *cold* out there. I've never seen weather like this in my life. All the records were broken last winter and now those too have been broken. That is if there was someone around to worry about keeping records."

Brian rubbed his eyes and sat at the dining table. "Well. Has the thief been back?"

"The eggs are gone and the ham and biscuits we left out."

"Then we're going to track him?" Brian seemed excited about a chance to do something different.

"After breakfast I am. You're staying here with the doors and windows locked."

"Shit. I haven't been out of this house in two days. It's boring as hell."

"Sorry, that's the way it's going to be. We know nothing about this person other than he hasn't done us any harm. Certainly, he's going to be uncomfortable about me trailing him. He's likely to shoot first and not bother to ask questions later."

"Is it worth the risk?" Brian got out of the chair and put more wood in the stove.

"That's a good question. But the fact is we need him if he's trustworthy. There hasn't been anyone around but him since those two men. But there will be sooner or later. We need another gun and farmhand."

"I thought you said people will be too weak from starvation to walk out here and the gas is running out."

Nate cracked eggs into a frying pan. "There might be a few that make it this far. And they might be the kind to take what they want...after they kill us."

"So you want me to stay here with the shotgun while you go off and get killed yourself." As he talked, Brian poured some water from a pail into a bowl in the sink and washed his hands in it.

Nate turned from the stove and glared at Brian. "That's not funny."

"I know it's not. I didn't mean it to be funny." Brian glared back. "You admit it's dangerous."

"Okay. Look. I'm the war vet here, and I think I've got a good chance of not getting myself killed. I've trailed better trained and armed people than this guy. And I'm your father. That means I'm the boss."

"You don't know."

"I know I'm your father." The tone of Nate's voice was calculated to let Brian know he was treading on thin ice. "And I am the boss around here. Fathers being the boss of their children is an old tradition. It's part of what a family is, and families are the building blocks of society. It's why God made fathers bigger than their children."

"I meant you don't know how dangerous he is. He might be some kind of Special Forces guy who went nuts and lives in the woods like a foamy-mouthed animal."

"Come on." Nate shook his head. "Your imagination is something. He seems to be going out of his way to *not* have a confrontation with us. He has not tried to harm us so far in any way, not even property damage. And I know he is good at surviving in the woods. I also know he's desperate, or he would never have come here. And he damn sure never would have kept coming back for our handouts. It could easily have been a trap."

"Yeah. We could have waited up and shot him like he was some kind of chicken thief."

Nate chuckled under his breath.

Brian enjoyed being a smart-mouth. Maybe it was a stage he was growing through. Usually his quips were amusing, sometimes even funny. Occasionally they were irreverent. But Brian knew there was a line that he could not cross without repercussions. Allowing Brian to be outwardly disrespectful would do harm not to the father, but the son. Nate never needed to control his children with fear; he used what he learned from his own father and his time in the military. If you want to receive respect, you first must teach them the meaning and value of respect by giving it to everyone in the family, including the children. Honor and respect is valued in the military, he saw no reason why that should change in civilian life.

"He only took eggs," Nate said. "Though he could have taken chickens before I locked the coop, but he didn't. Get the plates out while I cook. I want to be out there and trailing him as soon as I can see tracks."

"Eggs and wild hog again."

*   *   *

He was a smart one. Nate knew that already. *Trailing this guy is slow going. A blanket of snow on everything and still he is able to get down into the wet and leave no tracks. Poor bastard's boots must be full of ice water.*

Nate decided to go around behind the bayou and find where he came out. An hour and a half later, he began to think he was still in the water somewhere. There were no tracks. At least none he had been able to come across.

As the sun rose over the treetops, the wind picked up. It was blowing in his face. Little ice picks were pricking his nose and ears. It was probably still below twenty, and he couldn't move fast enough to keep his body heat up. Not if he wanted to sneak up on this...egg thief. And not if he was to have a chance of finding his trail again.

He thought he smelled something. *Smoke, hickory or oak.* He stood and finally decided it was definitely hickory. *Cooking. Or drying and warming his feet maybe. There's an island in that bayou, full of moccasins. Been there when I was a kid, hunting squirrels.* He searched the far side of water, peering through the scrim of trees. *I don't want to be wading in that in this cold. Snakes won't be a problem though. Damn it! I'll run back home and get waders. No. To hell with it. We left that sign before, then a note, asking why he doesn't introduce himself. We'll just write another note. If he still won't talk to us, I'll wait up for him some night.*

He shivered in the cold and headed home.

Nate stood at the back door. "Brian. Open up. He's in the Half Mile Bayou. That island I told you about." He heard Brian taking the steel bar down and working the locks.

Brian had a smile on his face when he opened the door. "Outsmarted you, huh?"

Nate locked the door behind him, savoring the warmth of the house and the aroma of bread baking in the oven. "You could say that. But it's more like he out-toughed me. I did not want to go wading in that ice water. We'll leave another note. If that doesn't do it, I'll waylay him some night when he shows to grab more food."

"Could be dangerous. You might have to kill him. He could start shooting."

"All true. I plan to be careful."

"I thought you were going to say that was good thinking." Brian had his mischievous smile on.

"Thinking things through before acting always is."

*   *   *

Brian looked in the wire box. "Food's still there. He hasn't been back in four days now."

"Damn it," Nate said. "Take it inside. We'll have those eggs, biscuits, and ham for breakfast."

Brian unlatched the door and pulled the food out. "Might as well stop leaving it."

"He'll come back. If he has not left the area. Hunger will drive him back."

They went inside the house and took their coats off.

"What do you think happened?" Brian asked.

"I know what happened. He knew I tracked him that morning. And he realizes I know where he's been hiding. That shook him. For some reason he still does not trust us. Yet he eats our food."

"Hell, we could have poisoned him if we wanted to hurt him." Brian grabbed a frying pan.

"He knows that. But hunger is a powerful force. For some reason he trusts us but only so far. Must be a reason for it, but I have no idea what it is." Nate got the coffee out of a cupboard. There was not much left, but he found another jar.

"Maybe he's mental or something," Brian said, just thinking out loud.

"Retarded? Crazy? No. He's just very careful...when he can be. If he was not starving, there is no way he would come within a mile of us. This guy is woods-wise, maybe military. He damn sure knew I trailed him. That means he checked his back trail sometime after I went home and found my tracks in the snow. I doubt he saw me. If he did, he's damn good and definitely military. And I mean elite military. My training isn't that rusty. And I've lived in these woods all my life. It snowed that night, so he checked his back trail before that. This guy is smart. And if he did see me, that means he could have shot me."

Brian gave his father a worried look. "What's the point in worrying about him? We have wasted enough time. Why the risk?"

Nate stood at the stove and sipped coffee. He savored it, knowing it may be the last jar. "Like I told you, we need help around here. We will just keep putting the food out, and if he starts coming back I will wait up nights in the barn. In the meantime, I will write another note and apologize for trailing him and explain we want to offer him a place to stay."

"Maybe he can't read." Brian sat at the table.

"Oh come on. He took the notes." Nate's eyes lit up. "Damn it. Why didn't I leave a pencil for him? I will ask him why he's afraid of us. Hopefully he will leave an answer on the note."

"Seems like we have gone through a lot of trouble for some stranger who is not grateful for our charity. I don't see where he's worth it." Brian walked to the stove to get hot water for coffee.

"Hasn't been much trouble yet," Nate said. "He didn't ask me to trail him, you know. The tricky part is when we meet face-to-face. Now *that* could be trouble."

"You got that right."

"Well, let's eat. We have work to do."

*   *   *

"I was wondering what you wanted the ladder for." Brian watched his father brush snow off their solar power array on the roof of the house with a broom. He was on a stepladder, but still having trouble reaching the far ends of the panels.

"I want to recharge that spotlight and some other batteries. And we might need to shoot at night. So I want to make sure I've got batteries for the Aimpoint on my M14. We'll run out of kerosene faster if we don't start using the twelve volt lights more and the lamps less. We have this small solar system, might as well use it to its fullest capacity. We're going to have to get better at conserving everything. From now on, we throw nothing away and waste nothing."

"We're living pretty damn low already, Dad. All we do is work. And we're eating wild hog every day, even though there's good food at Mel's. We don't even listen to the shortwave 'cause you're afraid I might hear something that will depress me. Like I don't have anything to bitch about already and I'm just a kid who can't handle anything."

Nate got down from the ladder. "I'm glad you don't bitch and complain. That could be tiresome."

"I wasn't bitching. I *am* tired of that shoe-leather hog though."

"What we didn't can will spoil when it gets hot, so we need to eat it now. Remember, we can't waste anything."

"Yeah, I know." Brian smiled. "I wonder how long before I'll have boar bristles coming out of my face like you."

Nate rasped his callused hands against his stubble. "That's not from eating hog. You'll be shaving in a couple more years. Once a week anyway."

"You growing a beard?"

"Just haven't shaved in a couple days. Probably cut it off tonight, if I have time."

"Makes you look like a bum." Brian smiled.

"Thanks."

"You're welcome."

"Nice way to talk to your father."

"I apologize. I shouldn't have said you're welcome that was too polite."

"Just for that, you can shovel the cow crap out of the barn."

"I do that every day anyway."

"And put a rope on her and put her in the pasture so she can walk around some. She's been in that stall too long."

"Must be nice to have a slave." Brian's tone made it obvious he was joking.

Nate folded the ladder and followed him into the barn. "Maybe if you get everything done, including your laundry, we will have time to go down to the river and catch some fish."

Brian's face lit up. "Fish is better than shoe leather hog."

Three hours later, Brian came out of the house, holding two fishing rods and a tackle box. He was able to get his clothes clean with water warmed on the wood stove. He hung them on a line behind the house.

Nate pumped more water with the hand pump for dishwashing after dinner. When finished, he picked up the bucket and saw Brian standing on the porch with the rods and a tackle box in his hands. "Hold your horses while I get my rifle and lock up. You need your coat too. It'll be colder by the time we get back." He took the bucket to the kitchen and set it down in front of the sink.

Brian leaned the rods against a wall and headed inside to his bedroom and grabbed his military surplus coat out of the closet. When he came out, he was also wearing the boonie hat his father gave him.

They walked down to the river. Nate was alert for any sign of people. It was not the egg thief he was worried about. His thoughts were on the fact they were exposed as they went about their daily routine of farm chores and trying to survive. It was impossible to maintain security and do the things necessary to keep from starving. Brian, he noticed, became more at ease with each week that passed since those two men came to kill them. This was both good and bad. Good for his psychological well-being and bad for his safety. He too, had become less diligent. But, goddamn it, he could not keep Brian locked in the house the next two or three years. Would it be that long? Or would it be even longer? He had no idea how long it would be before civilization pulled itself up out of the mud and came back to life. Until then, there would be no law and no justice but the bullet that comes out of your gun barrel.

Nate went the long way, skirting the field just inside the tree line, the way deer do, except at night when they feel safer. Brian noticed, and he knew Brian noticed. *A boy his age shouldn't have to worry about dying, about men coming to kill him.*

Brian caught the first bass. "It looks like about three pounds. Not too big to taste good. But I like smaller blues better."

Nate reeled his lure in. "Who doesn't like blues better? If you want small catfish, take that Rapala off and bait a hook with a piece of that pork and sink it in the deep hole by that log. It's been cold. But you might wake up a cat with that greasy meat."

"Okay. I'd rather have catfish than bass."

Glad to see Brian enjoying himself, Nate put his rifle by Brian on the log he was sitting on as he tied a hook and sinker on his line. "Keep this handy. It's loaded with the safety on. I'll be around the bend about thirty yards where that old snag churns the water up. I've caught a few bass there many a time. See anyone, grab that rifle and run for me."

"No one's coming out here." Brian tied a hook on while he talked. "Just about everyone is dead by now."

"I doubt that everyone's dead. We'll listen to the radio tonight, might learn something about what's going on in the world."

"Great. It's better than reading the same old books and outdoor magazines over and over." Brian looked up at his father, a mischievous gleam in his eyes. "Admit it: You want to catch bass for fun. And here I am fishing for food. You're just a big little boy."

"Don't worry, I'll eat the bass and you can have the catfish. But I haven't seen you bring one in yet. So far it looks like bass for supper, not catfish."

"Yeah, well, at least I caught something. Where's yours?"

"Under that snag." Nate started around the river bend where he could not see Brian. Subconsciously, he told himself it was only a few yards.

The largemouth bass hit his plug while he was jerking it along the surface so it would look like a wounded shiner. It hit hard, throwing water several feet, and fought for a few seconds before throwing the hook. Nate cast again, letting the current bring it under the overhanging log and into shade. It was still early enough in the afternoon the sun was bright. He stopped concentrating on the plug and looked around at the wintery scene. The naked branches of hickory, oak, and dead cypress forked upward, forming a scrim between his eyes and the bright blue of sky. A squirrel jumped from branch to branch, stopping to scold him for intruding, then jumping to the next tree and scurrying away. The snow had melted into the ground except under the shade of trees and brush, but it was already starting to get colder again as the afternoon faded. Finally doing something he and Brian did for enjoyment before the world went to hell made it seem like things were almost normal again. He was hoping this little diversion would be good for Brian, but found himself savoring the day too.

Nate's mind wandered back to before the plague, when his family was complete, and he realized once again how much he missed his wife and daughter. The plug was hit by a five-pounder and he returned to the present. Nate was enjoying the fight and starting to really relax for the first time in months. In the back of his mind, he thought he heard voices. The fish was getting his attention, and he did not let it sink into his consciousness. Brian must have caught a big catfish. Then one voice was louder and angry. Now he was sure. Dropping his rod in the mud, he ran for Brian.

A pistol shot rang out. It sounded like a .22 rim fire to Nate. He pulled his .44 magnum revolver as he ran. Brian was screaming.

Brian!

"Come out from behind that log kid and I'll let you live."

Brian answered, "Come and get me you bastard!" Nate's M14 boomed.

The .22 fired twice more.

Nate exploded from the brush. Two men, who were watching the log Brian was taking cover behind, the same log he was sitting on when Nate told him to keep his rifle close, heard him coming and turned to fire on him. One had what looked to Nate to be a cheap 22. rifle, the other a small pistol. Nate shot them both without taking time to aim, just looking over the sights, and shot them again as he ran past them and to Brian.

Nate scanned the area for more men, looking over the revolver's sights while holding it in the Weaver Stance, ready to shoot, but saw no one. "Brian, I'm coming up on you, don't shoot me."

Brian looked up from behind the log. "Did you get them?"

"Yes. How many are there?"

Before Brian could answer, Nate jumped over the log and snatched his rifle from Brian who was lying on his back. "How many are there?" He shouldered it and swung it in tandem with his eyes, swiveling his upper body as he searched for enemies.

"Two. I didn't see any others. They were in a canoe. One of them shot me."

Brian's words knocked the breath from Nate's lungs. He fell to his knees beside his son. "Where?"

He held his right foot up. "My leg. It hurts like fire."

His pant leg was soaked with blood. Nate quickly pulled it up the leg so he could see, with no concern for hurting him. Brian yelled from pain. The bullet went into the calf one inch from the back edge and out the other side. There appeared to be no blood vessels hit, and the wound was not near any bone. He moved Brian around so he could prop both his legs up on the log. Brian's face was contorted with pain. Nate's was wet.

One of the men started to scream. "Help me! Oh, don't let me die!"

Nate stood up, abject hate on his face. He walked over to the man who was holding his entrails in with both hands.

Nate stood over him, his eyes blazing. "You shot my boy, you son of a bitch!" He squeezed off two rounds into the man's chest, then turned and shot the other man twice more.

Brian kept talking all the way, explaining what happened, what the men said, and how one shot him as he dove behind the log and grabbed Nate's rifle. His words were not registering with Nate.

He looked up and saw his father crying as he carried him to the house. "I'm all right. I'm all right," he kept saying.

Nate did not hear. "I should never have left you alone. I let my guard down."

Once in the house, Nate put Brian on the dining table and rushed for the first aid kit. He used shears to cut his pants away and cleaned the wound. After laying Brian's leg on a clean towel he said, "Now just lie still and don't get it dirty."

Brian asked, "Aren't you going to sew it up or at least wrap it in a bandage? It's bleeding a lot."

"You haven't bled enough to cause problems, don't worry about that. It will stop bleeding now that you're not moving around. The wound will need to drain later though when it starts healing. The last thing it needs is to be closed up." His face was strained. "Your only real danger is infection. We're lucky it was just a .22."

Brian looked up at him. "There's no way you got it cleaned all the way through."

"The bullet probably pushed some small particles of your pants into the wound and there is a little bloodshot flesh around the exit. A doctor would probably cut some of that away. I have a scalpel, but I'm not about to try that. Just be still while I get your bed ready. Then I will bandage it."

Before he carried Brian to his bed, Nate bandaged his leg and gave him an antibiotic capsule his wife had been prescribed seven months before her death and just before the pandemic reached their county. She had cut herself and it became infected. She did not use all of them because the infection cleared up soon after. It was all he had. There were five capsules left.

"You can take another pill in the morning."

"Can I have a couple aspirin? It's hurting worse."

"It will thin your blood and make you bleed more. We used almost all of the non-aspirin stuff for your mother and sister." The look on his son's face caught his breath. "I'll give you two when I get back. That way you can sleep later. I need you awake for now."

"I know I'm supposed to be tough, but it hurts."

"You're not supposed to be anything but yourself. And I know it hurts like hell. Don't think that soldiers don't scream and cry when they're wounded; they do. When I'm gone, if you want to yell go ahead. Sometimes it helps take your mind off it."

"You were wounded."

"Yes. I'll be back as soon as I can."

"Did you yell out?"

"Yes."

"I bet you didn't."

"Your dad isn't as tough as you think. Maybe somewhere below half tough. I served with some who were though. Don't be worrying about how tough I think you are. You're my son and all I have; that puts you above everyone else in the world. I'm not trying to raise a tough son; I'm raising a good one."

Most of the pain washed from Brian's face for a few seconds. "Where are you going?"

"Back to the river."

"What are you going to do, shoot them again?"

"I would if they could feel it." Nate left the room.

Nate took the magazine out if his rifle and reloaded it from a military ammunition can on the floor of his closet. He stuffed another loaded magazine in his coat pocket even though he already had six magazines on his load-bearing harness.

Nate noticed Brian's pain had increased when he walked back into the room. "Be back as soon as I can, maybe forty-five minutes. I will get anything that might be useful and dump their bodies in the river."

"You can use one of their packs to carry their guns in." Brian tried to sit up.

"Hey. Don't move. Just lie still." Nate gently pushed him back down. Thinking of something, he brought a plastic trash can in from the kitchen and put it beside the bed. "If you get queasy, throw up in this. Don't worry if you miss. Just let it go and make sure you don't get any in your lungs."

"If I throw up the pills, they will do me no good." Brian held his stomach.

"That's one reason why I'm waiting to give them to you." Nate felt a little queasy himself. His hands had been shaking since he saw Brian was shot.

"I forgot to tell you they had a canoe," Brian said. "They came from downstream. There's more stuff in the canoe. Also, they talked funny, like they were from New Jersey or New York."

"Well, it's good you noticed details like that. It may make a difference some day if something else happens."

Brian rolled his eyes. "But not now, huh?"

"The main thing is there were only two of them. Right?"

"There were only two in the canoe for sure. And that's all I saw."

"And they're both dead, so they are no threat to us. By the way, you did tell me about the canoe. Now relax and I'll be back as soon as possible."

"Let me have the shotgun."

Nate handed it to him. "Remember, I'll speak up when I come through the back door as soon as I have it locked and barred again. When I get back I'll give you a couple pills. Tomorrow I will go to Mel's place. He probably has all kinds of painkiller stored away somewhere." Nate's face softened. "We've got enough for tonight so you can sleep." He started out the bedroom door.

"Bring back my two catfish and one bass I caught," Brian said. "I earned them and I'm damn sure going to eat them."

Nate suddenly stopped, turned, and looked at him from across the room. "I will cook them for you tonight if you're hungry. But I expect you'll be sleepy soon."

"This leg isn't going to let me sleep."

"You lost enough blood you'll sleep after the pills go to work." Nate left the room and locked the back door once outside.

At the river, Nate found both the .22 rifle and pistol had been taken. He looked up and down stream for a quarter mile, but saw no sign of the canoe. The bodies' clothes pockets were turned inside out and the wallets were lying on the ground beside them. Both contained money. He collected both his and Brian's fishing equipment and the fish. They were still alive. Brian had them on a stringer and left them in the water with the stringer tied to a root on the bank. The bass he was fighting when it all started had broken the line, but the rod and reel were still there. He took the wallets only to learn more about the men. After dragging their dead weight, one at a time, to the water and rolling them off the bank so the current could take them downstream, he gathered everything up and headed home. He felt eyes on him all the way.

Nate opened the back door. "It's me, Brian. You hear me?"

"Yes."

He put everything down, locked and barred the door, and went straight to Brian's room.

Brian quickly wiped his face. He said nothing.

Nate washed his hands and got the pills and a glass of water for him. After Brian took them, Nate said, "I'll clean and cook those fish for you. If you're still hungry."

"I…guess I should eat."

"Well, if you don't, what I don't eat can be put in the icebox."

The smell of frying fish wafted through the house. The sizzling kept Brian interested in supper, but when Nate mentioned he was baking biscuits Brian answered back, "I probably could eat."

Nate opened a can of beans. He spoke loud enough from the kitchen Brian could hear. "Someone took the guns and canoe. He took one of the men's packs too. In fact, he took about everything that could be useful for surviving. If those two had any extra ammo that was taken also. Their pockets were turned inside out."

"The egg thief?" Brian asked. He grimaced when he tried to move his leg to a more comfortable position.

"I would have to guess yes. Only useful items were taken. Their wallets were left beside the bodies. Both have quite a bit of money in them, a couple grand between the two of them. The most telling thing is nothing of ours was taken. The tackle was still there. And that certainly would have been useful to him. Seems to be a thief with his own brand of honor."

"He's a sneaky bastard," Brian said. "But he has been no use to us. He hasn't answered your notes offering him to join us, and he did nothing to stop them from shooting me."

"What could he have done?" Nate had to talk loud while he worked so his voice would carry down the hall. "He probably was not armed until tonight."

"Well, now he might shoot us both. He might even be the one who took our boat when the sickness first spread to this area."

"I doubt that," Nate said. "He hasn't been around that long. And so far the only thing he has stolen from us is eggs, and he could have taken a lot more. Everything else he has carried off, we gave him. The guns, canoe, and other things were taken from dead men. I wouldn't call that stealing. Those men certainly had no use for them."

Nate walked in the bedroom carrying a TV dinner tray with all the makings of a simple fish dinner. "We need to be more careful. Getting shot, even a little, is serious. We were lucky this time." He helped Brian sit up with his back against the headboard. "I have seen no reason to believe the egg thief is a danger to us, but we must be more careful."

Brian wiped his hands on his pants. "From now on I'm going to shoot first and ask questions later."

"We will talk more about that tomorrow. Wait and I'll get you a bar of soap and bowl of water to wash your fishy hands before you eat."

"The pills are working," Brian said, as he dried his hands on a towel Nate held out for him. "It only hurts like hell now."

Nate brought his meal in on another TV tray and they ate together in Brian's room. Nate spent most of the time making sure Brian had everything he wanted.

After Brian was finished, Nate took everything to the kitchen and cleaned up and washed dishes. An hour later, he walked into Brian's bedroom and found he had dozed off, at peace for now. Sitting in a chair a few feet from the bed, he thanked God, Brian was not hurting so much he could not sleep and began to think about how stupid he had been and how lucky he was that his son was not dead or dying. Plans he had made for the coming months were completely abandoned. There would be no fields plowed, no crops planted, not this spring. It was simply too dangerous for that now. As soon as Brian could walk, they would head for Mel's bunker. What's the point of growing food if you're dead from gunshot wounds before you can harvest it? Abandoning their farm meant their future food supply would be drastically reduced. That meant their survivability when Mel's food ran out would also be reduced. A man who liked to plan way into the future, he hated doing what he knew is the wrong thing under less dangerous circumstances. But he and Brian had to survive the next few months before they could survive the next few years. He sat there disgusted because he knew the ramifications of his decision were going to be painful and long-lasting.

When Brian woke three hours after sunrise, Nate was still there, watching him, thanking God for giving him another chance. It's more dangerous than he thought. Security is going to be number one from now on until he was sure the danger had diminished to a much lower level. He sighed. They had work to do, and Brian will be bedridden for many days.

Chapter 6

"Feel like eating breakfast?" Nate asked.

"Oh, I don't know. My stomach feels funny." His face contorted with pain. "I wish I could go back to sleep."

"You can sleep as much as you want. You're staying in bed anyway." Nate shifted uncomfortably in his chair. "I have decided we're going to move to Mel's bunker. It's just too dangerous to stay here and farm. Mel has enough supplies for several years, we will hide there until things settle down enough we can come back here and plant a crop. Maybe next year…or the next."

Brian's eyes grew round. "What about the cow, the chickens, all of our stuff here? Without us to guard the farm, someone will just move in or raid the place. We'll lose everything."

"That's—"

"Don't say it. I'm sick of your shit."

"What?"

"Lately you always say 'That's good thinking, Son.' Like you're teaching me or something."

Nate's eyes flared. "I am teaching you. I'm your father. And watch how you talk to me. I treat you with respect even though I'm a lot stronger and could easily bully you every minute of your waking days. But I do not talk down to you or demean you. How about returning the favor."

They both remained silent for several minutes, neither looking at each other.

Another outburst because things aren't going his way. His leg is hurting him. He doesn't want to leave the farm. So he takes it out on me. "Besides the fact I'm older and more experienced, I was trained by Uncle Sam and *do* have a lot to teach you. About things that can save your life. I know more about farming than you, and I damn sure know more about surviving a gunfight. I let my guard down and made some mistakes yesterday, but so did you. If just one of us had not screwed up, you would not be wounded, lying there and hurting." His eyes changed. "You could have been killed. All it would have taken was for that bastard to be a better shot."

"It wasn't your fault." Brian's expression changed from irritation to concern. "I should have had the rifle closer. I walked away from it to find a better place to cast from."

"That's what I mean: You made mistakes and so did I. We can't afford to make mistakes when our lives are at stake."

"Okay."

"And when you interrupted me, I was going to say what you said is correct. We will probably lose everything. Someone may even burn the house and barn to the ground after taking what they want."

Brian looked surprised. "Why would they do that?"

"Just because they can. Some people go nuts when there is no law to rein them in. I've seen it before. I've seen soldiers act like animals just because there was no one around to say they couldn't. Being hunted like an animal does something to you...and killing people. Part of it is the stress. Well, right now a lot of people are scared and hungry and cold and just plain fear for their life and their children. People do crazy things when they're like that."

"You mean like shooting me for no reason."

"Yes."

Nate stood. "I'm going to be busy getting things ready to move to Mel's. Today I'll be working inside, piling items I'll pack to Mel's first by the back door. If you get hungry or need anything, just speak up."

"I won't eat right now. Guess I should wait until you eat. Maybe by then my stomach will be better."

An hour later, Nate walked by the open bedroom door and was glad to see Brian sleeping again. He went back to stacking canned goods by the back door, most of which was food they had canned in Mason jars themselves.

*   *   *

Brian woke in the afternoon. He could hear his father working in the living room. Looking around, he noticed a stack of books on the floor near his bed. He reached down and picked up the one on top and read the title: "Small Unit

Tactics." *Maybe it'll take my mind off the pain.* He opened it and began to read.

*   *   *

"I was wondering if you're hungry now," Nate put two military surplus cans of ammunition down at his feet in the bedroom doorway.

"I can eat." Brian looked over the book at Nate. "Now that I know the difference between bounding overwatch and traveling overwatch, what good is it? This stuff is for a squad, we're just two people."

"A two-man team can use the tactics of fire and maneuver. One keeps the enemy's head down with covering fire while the other runs for cover and a better position. Same thing when one's weapon runs dry or has a malfunction. You yell out that you're loading and the other covers for you. We'll talk more about that stuff later."

"Seems like now would be a good time since I can't do anything 'cause of my leg."

"True for you, but there's plenty I can be doing. I already have the priority items piled by the back door and secondary stuff piled in the living room. You study while I cook, and we'll talk about any questions you have while we eat."

"Carrying all that stuff on our backs is going to take forever. And here I am with this leg." Brian's eyes lit up. "Why can't we make a raft and float it upriver? That would cut several miles off packing it on our backs."

Nate's mind began to work. "We have four fifty-five gallon drums and plenty of two by eight boards. If that old five horsepower kicker will run, we can just power upriver on the raft."

"Then there's about a mile of packing all that stuff through the swamp and then uphill through the forest to Mel's."

"It will take many trips," Nate said. "What we don't want is to leave a trail in the mud for anyone to stumble upon and follow right up to the bunker. That means I will have to take different routes to prevent my boots from cutting a deep trail in the mud and vegetation."

"You know, there's a creek that runs into the river. It comes close to Mel's place. We could have used that canoe, but the egg thief took it. He's getting to be more of a pain every day. And now he has two guns. Someday we're going to have trouble with him, just like those others."

"I still don't think the egg thief is a threat," Nate said. "But that canoe would have been perfect for the creek. It can handle about two hundred pounds with me in it. I could have just paddled right up the creek." Nate picked up two ammunition cans. "I guess I could make a smaller raft to transfer the load onto for the creek, and it will work as well as a canoe." He started for the living room. "I'll have something for you to eat in about thirty minutes."

* * *

Nate brought scrambled eggs to Brian.

"It's a little late for breakfast," Brian quipped. "But it's good anyway, especially since we didn't eat breakfast this morning."

"Might was well enjoy the fresh eggs. In a few days, we'll be eating the last we'll have for some time. After that, it will be Mel's powdered eggs for breakfast. The hens will have to be slaughtered since we can't take care of them."

Brian held a fork halfway to his mouth. "Why not?"

"Same reason we're moving to the bunker: We are easy targets while tending to stock. I thought we might be able to take care of them there, but have decided against it. So it will be chicken every day for a while soon."

"What about the milk cow?"

"Same thing." He saw Brian's reaction. "I know. That's why I waited so long to decide to move to the bunker. Once the hens and cow are slaughtered, that's it. No more milk or butter, no more eggs, just the powdered stuff at Mel's. It took you getting shot to force me to accept the price of abandoning our farm."

"How long will the seeds store?" Brian looked concerned. "I mean if we can farm again someday."

"A few years. Some will germinate many years from now. Mel has some stored in cans too." He saw the relief on

Brian's face. "And we can probably trade for some chickens and cattle. It's not the end of us farming you know. There are a lot of farms in this county, and many people will have livestock and seed to trade for things they need. Not everyone has died in the plague."

"I guess we have enough money to buy stuff from them even if the banks aren't open by then. There's that money in the men's wallets also."

"It's likely that money will be worthless until civilization is back on its feet. That could take years longer than I'm thinking we will have to stay in the bunker."

Brian was incredulous. "Money worthless! That's impossible. Isn't it?"

Nate left the room. He returned with the twenty-three hundred dollars the men had and put it on Brian's tray. "Want that to go with your meal? You can pretend it's lettuce."

Brian glanced down at the roll of cash and then up at Nate. "I know you can't eat money, if that's what you mean."

"That's right, you can't eat money. And which would you rather have in your hand if more men came to kill you, that roll of money, or your rifle?"

"I guess I could throw it at them, but I'd rather have my rifle."

"And what good is your rifle without ammunition?"

"It would just be a club."

"Right again," Nate said. "Under normal conditions money can buy you food, guns, ammo, chickens, cows, electricity, and heat for your home…whatever, but not now. And maybe not for many years."

A smirk spread across Brian's face. "I guess we're lucky to have a crazy survivalist like Mel for a friend."

"And you're lucky to have a crazy farmer father who reloads ammo and has enough reloading supplies to load thousands of rounds of common calibers. Among other needful things, ammo will be the new cash for sometime into the future."

"Oh, you've got ammo all right." Brian had his smart aleck face on. "We're rich just with .308, 44.mag, and 30/30 alone, and lots of .22s too. We're not so rich in shotgun ammo though."

"We've got about one hundred rounds of buckshot and fifty of number eight bird. We'll keep that for ourselves, but I can always farm your labor out as a plowboy. There are certainly not enough horses and mules in America to take the place of tractors once the gas and diesel runs out or goes bad. There will be plenty of people willing to trade a can of beans or something else they have for a month of you pulling a plow."

"Funny. You're hilarious." Brian rolled his eyes.

"Funny? I am serious. But you will be too busy on our farm by then."

"And what will you be doing?"

Nate looked him straight in the eye. "Someone has to walk behind the plow."

"I think you're right about everything being done by hand, but you will be the one pulling the plow 'cause you're bigger."

"Yeah, I'm bigger. And the one who's bigger makes the rules. All joking aside, the new economy is going to be based on barter and labor, not cash."

"What about gold? Mel said gold could be used in place of money if the world as we know it ended."

"When's the last time you had gold for lunch or used it to protect yourself?"

"Same as cash, huh?"

"If it was just a collapse of the monetary system, gold would still be valuable. But food and ammo would still be king, along with needful skills." Nate picked up Brian's tray. "We'll make it." He looked down at Brian, his face serious. "But we must be more careful from now on. Burn into your head that the next guy who gets shot will not be one of us."

As Nate walked out of the room carrying both their trays, Brian said, "Yeah, shoot first and ask questions later. It's like war."

"Not quite." Nate raised his voice so Brian could hear from the kitchen. "We don't want to be shooting anyone who means us no harm…or each other. You have the right idea. Just temper that attitude with common sense and total awareness of your surroundings. We must be alert at all times."

"Even while fishing."

"Yep."

"Even while sleeping," Brian joked.

"Especially while sleeping."

"One of us has to pull security while the other sleeps?"

"Sometimes." Nate dropped a dish in a bucket of water to rinse. "Pull security? You've been studying my books; keep at it while you're stuck in bed."

"Nothing else to do."

Nate walked back into the bedroom. "Actually, starting today, you will be guarding the house while I'm working on the raft."

Brian pulled himself against the headboard so he could use it for a backrest. "From bed? How?"

"Let me show you. I'll be back in a minute."

The sound of a bed being dragged across Nate's bedroom floor screeched through the house. Then Brian heard a bolt-action rifle being worked open and closed.

Nate returned and stood by Brian. "Okay, I'm going to help you to my room. We'll take it slow and careful." He bent down and lifted Brian's legs and let them dangle from the edge of the bed. Then he lifted his upper body. "Don't use your leg at all, just the other one. Careful you don't bump it."

Brian grimaced. "It hurts already. I was shot last night, not last week."

"I know, but we must start packing everything to Mel's now. It's going to take days as it is. I would carry you, but that will put more strain on your leg than just doing it this way."

With Nate in the lead, Brian was bodily carried down the hall. Brian held his wounded leg up as his other foot slid down the hallway, barely touching, his lips tight, eyes slits. When he could take no more, he said, "It hurts."

"Almost there."

When he was in Nate's bed, back against the headboard with pillows behind his back and head, the relief rushed across his face.

Nate put another pillow under his leg. "It's bleeding a little." He watched Brian wipe sweat from his forehead with a sleeve. "Sorry, but it was necessary."

Brian blew out a lung full of air. "You didn't even ask if I *wanted* to be moved."

"There was no need to ask, I knew you didn't want to leave that comfortable bed. Like I said, it had to be done. There are three more of those pills."

"I don't need any goddamn pills. I can take it if you can."

Nate stayed calm. "Do you think I like seeing you in pain? I need you here looking out that window." He handed Brian 10x50 Zeiss binoculars. "Can you see the river from here?"

Brian rolled his eyes. "You know we can't. The river valley is at least thirty feet lower than here."

"Use the binocs and scan the tree line on both sides of the field and learn how far you can see into the shade of the trees. Then learn how far towards the river you can see from here."

Brian blew out another lung full of air and wiped more sweat from his face. "Why?"

"Because it could save my life."

Brian blanched and took more interest in the binoculars. Concern for his father overcame the pain of is wound, but he was still angry and it showed. Then he picked the binoculars up and looked through them, sweeping the scene he could see through the window.

With no sign of losing patience, Nate said, "You're going too fast. Go slower, a lot slower. Examine every detail back in the trees. I'll go get you a pill."

Brian jerked the binoculars down and glared at his father. "I told you I don't need any goddamn pill!"

"Cool it. Taking a pill doesn't make you weak. Striking out verbally because you're in pain *does* show weakness and immaturity. There have been plenty of times when I was irritated, tired, worried, or whatever, when I could have taken it out on you, your sister, or mother, but I controlled myself because it would be wrong. If you want to show me how much of a man you are, start with that. If this wasn't important, you would still be in your own bed. I'm sorry as hell you're hurting. Now when I get back, you're going to take a pill. That leaves two more in case you need them later. Meanwhile keep learning how to use those binocs. I mean really learn how to use them. I'm going to have to pack everything to the river on my back. It's going to take many, many trips. I will need you overwatching with the Remington, protecting me."

Anger faded on Brian's face. "Okay. I guess I was blaming you for my leg hurting. You didn't seem to care."

"That's bullshit and you know it." Nate left the room, his own temper rising. *Don't care?*

Brian put the binoculars down when Nate returned with a glass of water and the pill bottle. "I'm too far back from the window. I could see more if I was closer."

"It's safer where you're at. A sniper never shoots with his barrel sticking out the window. They can't see you back from the opening. The muzzle flash won't give you away unless it's night, and it will be harder to locate you by the rifle report."

"Will shooting through glass throw the bullet off?"

"Yes. The first shot anyway. But the glass is gone. It will be cold with the shutters open."

"I was thinking about other windows," Brian said. "Just give me my sleeping bag. I'll be okay."

"I'll leave the dining room shutter and window open too. Otherwise they will notice this window being the only open one and know where you're shooting from."

Brian took another sip of water. "But they can get in that way."

"I will stretch barbwire across it on the inside. All they will see is the window is open until they try to get in."

"What if they cut it?"

"They're not likely to have wire cutters with them. And I will be out there with my rifle." Nate pulled a chair up to sit beside Brian. "Look, chances are we'll be out of here before anyone else shows up. It's just that I will be vulnerable while packing all that stuff to the river and need you looking out for me with that rifle." He tried to give Brian a reassuring smile. "But today I'll be in the barn cutting lumber for the raft. I've got to get the torch out and weld brackets to those drums too. I've seen people use cable to attach drums to the bottom of floating docks, but I will use bolts through the brackets."

"So you want me to just sit here glassing the tree line and field?"

"If you keep at it long enough," Nate said, "you will learn just how far back into the shade of those trees you can see with quality binocs. That's where they're most likely to be shooting at me from." He stood. "I'll be back in a few minutes to show you a range card I drew for you."

"Range card? What's that?"

"I will show you. But first I have to bring a heavy sheet of steel in from the barn. I think it's about the right size to put between you and the window for armor."

"Jeez." Brian opened his eyes wide.

"Yes. It may all be overkill, but I don't want any more holes in you. It won't be complete protection. I wish it were, but you can't shoot without exposing your upper body. Now we've both been shot, me years ago, you yesterday, that's enough."

"Better safe than sorry," Brian said.

"Yes. Better safe than dead."

It took Nate fifteen minutes to carry the steel plate out of the barn and through the house to the foot of the bed. After catching his breath, he said, "This thing weights at least two hundred pounds."

"I wish I could help," Brian said. "And I hope you're keeping your eyes open while you're out there."

"I am. But you're watching this side of things. That reduces my worries fifty percent. It's a lot easier for me to keep watch on just one side of the farm. The back of the house is not under watchful eyes though. Full security is impossible with only two people."

"I wish Mel was here."

Nate walked outside without a word, but thinking the same thing. He brought several solid concrete blocks in to set against the steel plate, leaving the plate held up by the foot of the bed on Brian's side and the blocks on the other. He pushed against it with both hands. "A common deer rifle won't knock this over, especially from long distance."

Brian stopped glassing the scene through the window. "You were going to show me a range card."

"First I have to make a shooting bench for you so you can use the bipod on the Remington." Nate picked up the bolt-action and worked the bolt back. "See, it's not loaded. Now practice looking through the scope at long range. Dry fire it too, for practice. When I get back, I want you to tell me how far away that tall dead pine is on the left edge of the field. Also the big oak in the right corner, and that water tank in the cow pasture, and how far can you see a man lying in the field towards the river."

"Geez," Brian said, "you're serious about this."

"I'm serious about keeping us alive. I was hoping you would have no need to know how to use a sniper's rifle, but that went out the window months ago." Nate took a measuring tape out of his pocket and took note of how high to make the shooting bench and how wide.

Brian watched. "You're going to make the legs tall enough it will stand on the floor and not the mattress?"

"The mattress shakes too much."

"Oh, right."

Nate came back with what looked like a tall sawhorse made of two by sixes. He was forced to maneuver it through the door as it was a tight fit with the legs more than three feet apart and the ridge board five feet long. He came back a few minutes later with the second one. Then he carried in a piece of three-quarter-inch plywood and nailed it on the sawhorses while Brian sat there watching. He lifted the side nearest him until it fell on its end on the other side of the bed. "That's how we'll get it out of the way so you can get out of bed fast if need be." He leaned over the bed, grabbed the nearest leg, and pulled the shooting bench back in place. "Gotta get one more item."

Nate left the room again and returned with a shooting bag filled with sand, placing it in front of Brian on the bench. "I taught you how to use a shooting bag, so go to it. Aim for that water tank. Pretend there's someone shooting at you from behind it on the right end."

"Okay." Brian positioned the bag where he thought it should be and placed the rifle so it would point in the general direction of the water tank while the heel of the rifle's butt was on the bag. Then he squeezed the bag with his left hand to raise or lower the butt of the rifle and adjust elevation. He adjusted the rifle's position, aimed, held his breath, and squeezed the trigger.

"You did one thing wrong."

Brian looked up at Nate. "What's that?"

"The pillows on the headboard are fine for a backrest when you're just looking or resting, but you need to lean forward when shooting and forget those pillows behind you."

"Why? It seemed steady that way." Brian seemed puzzled.

"When the rifle recoils, your upper body must roll with it a little, or it will hurt. It can't move if it's back against the headboard. I'll go get your insulated vest. It will act as a recoil pad. You will be cold with the window open anyway."

"I don't remember this gun kicking that bad when you let me shoot it."

"It doesn't," Nate said. "The rifle is heavy with a long barrel, so it doesn't kick much. It's just a .308. But you do not want to be shooting it with your back up against that headboard. Just lean forward a little, about an inch or so, when you shoot and it will not hurt at all."

"Okay. You're the boss."

Nate smiled. "About time you realized that."

Brian rolled his eyes. "Yeah, yeah. You know, it's going to be loud in this room, my ears will be ringing, and I will be deaf after the first shot."

"You're right. I should have thought of that. I'll go get your vest and the electronic shooting muffs. The batteries are still good. And I'll get mine and keep them handy too. Then we will be able to hear each other in a gunfight and not be deafened by the gunfire."

Yelling through the open door and down the hall, Brian said, "And when are you going to show me what a range card is?"

"Hold your horses." Nate yelled from his bedroom closet. "That's next. We're about to get into the serious business of long-range shooting. For now, just practice dry firing on that water…that boat in the cow pasture."

"What? What boat?" Brian shook his head and looked out the window at the pasture several hundred yards away. "Is this some kind of test, or are you crazy?"

Nate put the shooting muffs on the plywood by the rifle and handed Brian his vest. "I just woke up and realized that galvanized steel water tank out there will make a boat for transporting hundreds of pounds of stuff upriver."

Brian's eyes lit up. "Damn! Why didn't I think of that?"

"Yeah, why didn't you?"

"Oh, shut up." Brian waved him off with a smile.

"If the kicker will run, I can load it up and power right up the river with it. It's long and narrow, only about three feet wide and fifteen feet long, so I will need to stabilize it with a drum on each side. That way I can stack the load high and not worry about capsizing. The thing to do is make several trips and unload at the creek. On the last river trip, I will take the drums off and carry smaller loads up the creek. The tank being so narrow will be an asset then, as the creek is choked with fallen limbs and weeds. I will have to pole it through all that and leave the motor at the river. It's still a lot faster than packing it on my back all the way."

"I just hope we're left alone long enough to get all this done and moved to Mel's."

Nate became somber. "Chances are we will be, but I wouldn't count on luck."

Brian sighed. "My leg hasn't been hurting since you started making me into a sniper. It keeps my mind busy. Now, what is a range card?"

Chapter 7

Brian checked the range card Nate drew for him and read that the tall dead pine tree on the left edge of the field was five hundred and fifty-three yards from his rifle. The rock he was using for a target was about fifty yards closer. He then determined he needed to aim one half a Mil Dot low at that range by checking a card Nate had made up showing the holds, or aiming points, at various ranges. He held his breath and squeezed the trigger.

The rock sparked in the shade of trees in the sunless afternoon, and powdered rock produced a puff of dust.

"Perfect!" Nate was watching through binoculars. "Now hit that stump near the right corner of the field. It's in the shade and hard to see." He handed Brian the binoculars. "Hurry, it's getting late and this will be your last target. The next time you shoot from here, it will be at a man."

Brian searched the dark tree line. "What stump? How far out?"

"Eight hundred: the limit of your rifle's reach. It's to the right of where a hog rooted. Hurry."

Again, Brian checked the range card to confirm it was eight hundred yards away. He had been tricked by his father before and was not going to fall for that again. Checking the holds card told him he needed to hold three Mills high. He handed the binoculars to Nate and aimed, fired.

The stump exploded into powdered punk wood.

"Great shot! Your old man will live another day."

Brian blanched. He took off his earmuffs, set them on the plywood, and looked out the window at the darkening dusk.

Nate took his earmuffs off and turned the switch to save batteries, then did the same for Brian's. "Reload." His voice was hard. "This isn't a game. We're trying to stay alive. Why do you think I spent all afternoon with you and used so much ammo?"

"I know."

"The weight on your shoulders is heavy. You're wondering what if you miss. Well, that's the way it is. Just remember I will love you no matter what. You are my son. Just do the best you can. You do that by staying calm and relying on what I've taught you. Panicking will just get us both killed."

Brian pushed a round into the rifle. "I didn't panic when the boar charged."

"No you didn't. It was a close shot but a moving target that must be taken out fast is actually harder to execute properly than a long shot when you have plenty of time. If I didn't think you could do it, I would not have spent so much time on this."

Brian sighed. "Okay."

Nate pulled up a chair and sat. "Look, chances are no one will come around before we're out of here. Shouldn't take more than about five days for me to get it done. It would have been ten times that long without the river and creek. The next people to show up will probably be starving beggars, and not dangerous. We will just give them some of that boar and send them away."

"But you don't know."

"That's right. For all we know, ten armed killers *may* show up. It's not likely, but it could happen, so we must be as ready for trouble as we possibly can."

Brian's chest rose and fell, but he said nothing.

Nate stood. "Let's get this stuff out of the way so you can lie down while I cook something for supper. I will start packing to the river at first light. That means we must get up at least an hour before that so we'll have time to eat and set you up here. Once I start packing, I will not be stopping until it's too dark to see."

"When are you going to get the water tank?"

Nate closed and latched the shutter and closed the window. "Tonight after we eat. You will be watching from that bed."

Brian's eyes narrowed from nervousness. "What can I see in the dark?"

"You can see better than you think through the binocs and scope. I will stay in contact with you through those handy talkies your mother bought so she could keep track of me while I worked the farm." His eyes became distant for a few seconds. "She was always afraid I would fall off the tractor or cut a leg off with the chainsaw or something. I'll be telling you where I am every step, so you won't shoot me."

"Damn it, Dad! That's crazy."

Nate's voice hardened again. "I will go down the left side of the field just in the trees and come straight across the pasture to the tank. Anyone shoots at me from the other side of the field or from the direction of the river, kill him. Now that's simple, isn't it?"

"Yeah, simple. Why not wait until daylight?"

"I don't want anyone to see me dragging that tank to the river. They will know what I'm planning. And it will be more dangerous in daylight. I will be in the middle of the pasture and an easy target. It's going to take some time for me to dip enough water out before I can lift it to turn it over and drain the rest. I'd rather do that in the dark."

"Okay, if it must be tonight. Just keep telling me where you are with the radio."

After dinner, Nate helped Brian get ready to overwatch from the window.

"Ready?" Nate asked.

Brian pulled the rifle's bolt back far enough to see if it was loaded. "Which way are you going to drag the tank down to the river?"

"Down the left side of the field. I can't get that thing through the trees, so I'll have to stay in the open on the edge."

"You will be making a lot of noise."

"Yes," Nate said.

Brian looked at his father. "And your hands will be busy, so your rifle will be slung on your back."

"That's why I'm doing this tonight and why we went through all the preparation. There's going to be days of this. Tonight will be over in about an hour. The next five days will be from first light to last."

"And if no one shows up, it will all be a waste."

Nate tried to read Brian's face. "And if someone dangerous does show, it could save both our lives."

"I know." Brian's chest deflated. "Wouldn't it be nice if the world didn't have so many assholes in it?"

Nate laughed. "They're being thinned out by people like us as we speak."

"You got four of them yourself."

"Well, you're all set here, and the shotgun is on the bed with you in case someone gets close or breaks in. I'm heading out. Stay alert and have confidence in yourself."

Brian turned the radio on. "Okay."

Nate made his way in the dark, keeping to the shadows. His military training told him shadow is life, along with silence and slow, fluid movement. Safer still, is no movement at all, but he had a job to do.

The night was clear and growing colder. A milky cloud of stars felt so low and close, he felt the need to duck. He could see nearly across the pasture, bathed so intensely in the starlight, even a coyote caught his eyes as it dashed for the woods. His rifle in his right hand, a black five-gallon plastic bucket for bailing the tank out in his left, he stalked on, clinging to the shadows.

The radio squawked and Brian's voice pierced the silence. "I saw something moving fast on the other side of the pasture!"

Nate stopped. Put the bucket down, and pulled the radio out of a jacket pocket. "I saw it." He whispered into the microphone. "It was a coyote. I'm about halfway to where I'll start out across the pasture. Stay off the radio unless it's an emergency."

Nate moved on approaching the edge of the pasture when he heard something move in the brush farther back in the trees. He stopped to listen, though he was certain it was a possum or some other small animal. He stood there for five minutes, just listening and peering into the dark under the canopy of trees.

Nothing.

Nate took one step.

"Don't shoot. I mean you no harm." A girl's voice, low in decibels, but clear, came out of the dark.

Nate was startled. A girl was the last thing he expected. He did not speak or move except to slowly lower the bucket and bring his rifle to his shoulder.

"I wanted to thank you for the food," the girl said, "especially the eggs, since I didn't ask when I took them. I don't like stealing, but I was hungry."

Nate still said nothing. He stood and tried to locate her.

"Is the boy okay? I saw you carry him home and haven't seen him out of the house since. I don't blame you for killing those men. They had items in the canoe they took off other people. Probably they killed them. How is the boy?"

Nate stepped behind a thick pine tree. "He's okay."

"Good."

Nate began to get an idea where she was. "Why haven't you answered my notes, my offer for you to join us? You would be a help, not a burden."

"Lots of reasons. You know. It's dangerous. Besides."

"Besides what?"

"I'm a girl."

"I'm not interested in hurting you."

"Your offer was for a man; you don't think I can carry my weight."

"My offer is for you—man, woman, boy, or girl. Anyone who can survive alone with no shelter like you is an asset. All we ask is you be honest with us and do us no harm."

"I want to trust you, I guess I should, you've helped me. But people are hurting one another now. I learned not to trust anyone."

"Is there anything you need? Warm clothes perhaps. We have a lot of extra items like sleeping bags and clothes. My wife's clothes may fit you."

"A...a sleeping bag...and something for rain."

"A poncho? We have plenty of those."

"Yes."

"We'll leave it out behind the barn."

"I won't get it tonight. You'll be waiting for me."

"No we won't. But you should stay away for now. We're jumpy and might shoot before we know it's you. Come back some other night. It's dangerous tonight."

"Why?"

"If you want to know our plans, you first have to join us. Trust works both ways. I'll leave a note in the box explaining when it's safe to come and get what we leave for you. Just stay away tonight, or you might get shot."

"All right."

"And think about joining us," Nate said. "You have a few more days to decide."

"Why a few days?"

"I've got to go now. You should go back to your camp and think about joining us."

Nate heard little noise as she slipped away into the night. Standing in the silent dark, he hoped she would do what he said.

This thing is going to kill me. Nate pulled on the water tank, dragging it a few more yards before stopping to rest his tired back and arms. He could not wait to get the damn thing to the slope where it will be downhill to the river swamp. But then there will be brush and trees to deal with.

*   *   *

Brian glassed into the starlit night, meticulously searching deep into every shadow along the right edge of the field. Occasionally, he scanned the field and pasture in case someone came out of the woods on the left. Three hours had passed since his father walked into the woods. As time ticked by and nothing happened, his nerves calmed, but now he wondered what was taking so long.

Every time an urge to call on the radio overtook him, he remembered his father telling him to stay off the radio unless it was an emergency. If he hit the transmit button at the wrong time, such as if his father were hiding silently in the dark, he could get him killed.

Brian jumped when the radio screeched and Nate's voice boomed in the bedroom. "I'll be coming in the backdoor in a minute." He took the radio off his lap and started to speak but realized it was unnecessary. He would just wait for his father to walk into the room before he asked what the hell took so long.

Nate appeared at the bedroom door drenched in sweat, despite the cold. "I only got it a little way into the swamp before I had to quit." He plopped down on a chair. "Didn't realize how heavy that damn thing is. Dragging it through brush and cypress trees when I got out of the field and into the swamp finished me. I left it hidden in brush."

Brian was silent.

Nate closed the shutter and window. Sitting on the chair again, he noticed Brian was still wound up but holding it in. "I had a talk with our mysterious friend, the egg thief."

"You're pulling my leg." Brian, annoyed, leaned forward. "You could have picked the radio up and told me why it was taking so long." He crossed his arms and stared straight ahead.

"It would have just brought more risk to us both." Nate was slightly amused at Brian crossing his arms and almost pouting. "The less noise I made out there the better, same for you." He stood. "I'm worn out, and I need a drink of water. You want anything while I'm in the kitchen?"

"No."

Nate yelled from the kitchen. "What I said about having a chat with the egg thief is true." He returned and leaned against the bedroom doorframe, holding a glass of water. "And you won't believe this, but the thief is a girl."

Brian snorted. "You're right: I don't believe it."

"Never saw her in the dark woods, but from her voice, I'd say she's a teen, a little older than you."

Finally realizing his father just might be telling the truth, Brian searched his face for any evidence of an impending "gotcha." He saw none. "Come on! A girl living out there in the woods? In this cold? With no shelter or food other than our eggs and wild rabbits?"

"We did leave more than eggs for her. Impressive though, isn't it? She's one tough girl. Probably looks like a cave woman or sasquatch though."

"If you're telling the truth, what did she say?"

"Asked about you. Evidently she saw me carrying you to the house after the fight. Knew you hadn't been out of the house since. I tried to convince her we mean her no harm, but she's really suspicious and careful. My guess is she's seen a lot of violence in town and doesn't trust anyone. Probably lost her family in the chaos."

"Is that all? You didn't learn anything else about her?"

"She did ask for a sleeping bag and rain gear. I told her we would leave it out for her. Now I'm thinking we should leave a box of .22 hollow points, one of your mother's coats, and a tarp."

"She's stupid if she won't trust us."

"I wouldn't say that. No telling what she's been through. We're kind of jumpy since you got shot. Hell, we're leaving a perfectly good farm because of it. In fact, I told her to be careful because we might shoot her after the trouble with those last two."

"You told her right." Brian looked straight ahead. "She better not be sneaking around at night anymore."

"By the way, she apologized for stealing the eggs, said she was hungry."

"I bet she was. I bet she's hungry now."

"Feeling sorry for her?"

Brian snorted. "I was just saying."

*   *   *

Nate yelled from the kitchen. "Time for breakfast. We have to hurry because I want to be in the woods with my first load of the day just as soon as there's enough light to see."

Brian groaned and pulled the cover over his head when the smell of coffee and frying sausage refortified his ambition to do his part. He yawned, stretched, sat up, and reached for his warm vest. Still cold, he pulled on a coat and buttoned it.

"How's your leg?" Nate put Brian's breakfast on the shooting platform. It made a prefect table.

Brian took a sip of coffee. "Doesn't hurt anymore. Feels funny."

Nate's eyes flashed to the bandaged leg. "I should have checked it yesterday." He put his fork down, still full of scrambled egg, and stood. He had Brian's breakfast off the shooting platform and the platform tilted over out of the way in seconds.

Irritated, Brian asked, "What did I say? I'm hungry, damnit!"

Nate nearly tore the wet bandage off, cutting with a small pocketknife. His face suddenly lost all color. The leg was hot to the touch, the wound red and swollen. Fluid oozed onto the towel under Brian's leg. Nate's chest deflated. He turned his face from Brian so he would not see. Rushing out of the room, he said, "I'm going to get the medical kit." When he got down the hall, he stopped, braced himself with a hand against Brian's bedroom door; he needed support to keep from falling over. The world was spinning around his head. Smearing tears from his face, he stiffened and returned with the medical kit he knew did not contain what he needed to save Brian's life.

"Damnit, that hurts!"

"Sorry, but it must to be cleaned." Nate scrubbed the wound with antibiotic-soaked gauze. When he was finished, he put a clean towel under Brian's leg and left it uncovered so it could drain. He wiped his forehead with a sleeve. "If you're still hungry, I'll put the platform back in place so you can finish breakfast."

"It's cold by now."

"I'll warm it for you."

"No, I'll eat it cold. You're already sweating, even in this cold room. You don't need to be standing over the stove."

"I'm just tired." Nate pulled the shooting platform back in place and set Brian's food on it.

"You just woke up," Brian said. "I'm not stupid. I can see you're worried."

Nate looked at his hands to see if they were shaking. "You're okay. I just should have been checking the wound instead of packing to move."

"There's nothing you can do, even if you cleaned it every hour. Stop blaming yourself. You didn't shoot me."

Nate's eyes flashed to Brian. He forced himself to swallow. "I'm going to Mel's today. He's bound to have more drugs than we have."

"Don't do that. Just keep packing stuff to the river."

"Not that you have a vote, why?"

"More people will be coming. Not just from town, but even from the nearest cities. You need to be at Mel's as soon as possible."

"*We* need to be there. You're one hell of a long way from dead, Brian. It's just starting to fester a little. Mel is bound to have some stronger drugs. Anyway, we'll know in a few hours."

"Yeah, that's why you're as white as a sheet. You look like you did when Beth first got sick."

Nate blanched, his eyes flared as he stared Brian down.

"You just turned whiter."

"You're making me angry. Stop it. You're not dying." Nate's face washed over with realization. "Do you *want* to live?"

He did not answer.

"Brian, answer me!"

"I don't want to leave you alone." He turned his head to stare at the far wall. "It wouldn't be fair to let you have all this fun to yourself."

"So you're feeling sorry for yourself again. You know what keeps me going? You. Try caring for someone other than yourself. It puts things into perspective."

Brian turned his gaze back to Nate, his eyes red. "You were a good husband for Mom and a good father for Beth and me. I know that."

"It will get better in time. There is a life ahead for you. That's what I'm working for. We just have to make it through this. Right now you're health is number one."

"I wasn't talking about me."

"I am."

"Okay. Since you want to talk about me, just know I don't want to lose my leg. What good will I be in this world we're in now with one leg? It's my leg, my life, and my choice."

Nate's anger boiled over. "Shut up! You're just a kid. And now all of a sudden you decide to play some character you read about. You've seen too many movies. You would bleed to death or die of shock anyway. Stop that shit. It's nowhere near that bad. Mel has drugs. Hell, he stockpiled everything else." He sighed as his eyes roamed around the room, desperately searching inwardly. "The drugs will be out-of-date, but they should still be okay to use."

"I've been thinking about what could happen while lying here since I was shot. So I didn't just come up with this now. And I didn't read I was going to get shot in a book or see it in a movie. It's my right. You have to promise you won't do it without my permission."

"Will you shut up? We're a *looong* way from that. I told you you're going to be okay. And you are still just a kid, and I'm your father. I am telling you to stop thinking like that. You will be okay. If that changes, I won't lie to you."

"Okay."

Nate stood. "I need to start for Mel's now." He left the shotgun beside Brian on the bed. "You can sleep. If someone tries to break in, they will have to make more than enough noise to wake you."

"Just don't run all the way there and give yourself a heart attack."

Nate was quiet for thirty seconds. It took him that long to calm down. He wanted to punch Brian out. No. He wanted to hold him and tell him he would have him in a hospital in less than an hour. He wasn't angry with Brian; he was mad at the world. He hated the men who shot him. He hated that Brian was forced to grow up in a matter of months.

"No, I will have to take my time to avoid blundering into an ambush. Might be more criminals around."

Brian seemed glad to change the subject. "Criminals? They're just regular people who don't care anymore. Hunger and fear turns people into animals."

Chapter 8

Nate was in rough country, about two thirds of the way to Mel's cache, when he first heard them coming. Three men, stumbling through the woods, announcing their arrival seventy yards ahead of them with all the noise they made, bitching at each other about how cold, tired, and hungry they were.

As they went by, Nate hid behind a limestone rock next to a bushy, short magnolia and listened. They were too far to see through all the brush, but their loud voices carried across the still air. Nate recognized that, they were city people, with no idea of how to travel quietly in woods.

They must think they're the only ones in the county. Damn fools aren't going to live long.

"We'll camp by the river, might rob a family coming up from town," one gravelly voice said.

The one who had been quiet until now spoke up. "Maybe we should wait until the others get here."

A third voice responded angrily. "You gutless bastard! It doesn't take seven men to do that."

"I just don't see any reason to bother with some family traveling the river by boat. They're not likely to have much. Once the others get here, we can take the Williams farm like Chuck said, and we'll be set with all we need. Then we can rob everyone who comes up or down river."

Nate's mind raced. The only Chuck he knew was from high school. A kid from a family of convicts who was fast following his two big brothers' and father's path. He had been in trouble since the age of ten and by fifteen had graduated to armed robbery, general thug activity, and drug dealing. Last Nate heard Chuck was serving life in state prison for murder. That was eleven years ago. Why would escaped convicts come all this way?

He remembered they lived in a notorious neighborhood of rundown trailers and shacks known as "White Trash Hollow," where spouse and child, as well as alcohol and drug abuse, were rampant. He nearly beat Chuck Shingle to death one day after a baseball game when he tried to force himself on the girl Nate would later marry. It was the fact Nate was preventing a "forcible felony," which, under state law, made it legal to use deadly force that stopped the state from charging him with attempted murder. When it came out during sworn testimony that Chuck was the first to use the bat, breaking two of Nate's ribs and his left arm, all the lesser charges were also dropped. Nate's clean record and Susan's testimony also helped.

The fight left Chuck Shingle's face deformed for life.

Shingle became the laughingstock of the county when he pled to the judge during sentencing that he was not at fault because "alcohol was involved." The judge responded. "It usually is." Shingle was never charged with attempted rape or assault with a deadly weapon. At first, it appeared Nate was going to be in more trouble than Chuck. In the end, Nate's charges were all dropped and Chuck got six months for assaulting Susan. Nate stormed out of the court. When asked by a reporter what he thought about the sentence, Nate replied, "The next girl he attacks better not be Susan. And there *will* be a next."

Three weeks after Chuck Shingle was released from prison, nearly two months early for good behavior, two of the Williams' cows were shot with a hunting bow as they grazed near forest land on the edge of the pasture. A month later, all their vehicles were sabotaged with sand in the gas tanks. That summer, the barn was partially burned one night before the Nate family could put it out. They lost all their hens and two roosters.

Nate was losing sleep, staying up nights with his father's double-barrel shotgun and was worried sick Shingle would harm Susan. But Susan was never bothered again by Chuck Shingle. Her father caught Shingle drunk and alone one night. By daylight, the fear of God was permanently implanted in his brain. He came close to dying, and had collected more facial scars to go with those Nate gave him. He was afraid to file a complaint. If he wanted Susan, he had better kill her father first. And then there was Nate. In a rare spark of common sense and sanity, he told everyone who would listen he considered the matter closed and would never bother Susan or the Williams family again. Everyone knew why, but knew better than to antagonize him by rubbing it in.

"Likely be a wife and daughter with them," the gravelly voice barked. "You remember what a woman is, don't you? Or have you been everyone's cell bitch so long you forgot?"

"Yeah, asshole, you've been nothing but a whining pussy since we broke out," the second voice added. "When Doug killed that deputy last week, you kept whining about the death penalty."

"I might be a pussy, but you'll be the one whining when they strap your ass down and shove that needle in. Just because there's no law now doesn't mean this country won't get back on its feet someday."

"See what I mean?" The gravelly voice sounded letdown. "I told you he would just be dead weight. Here we are in a hunter's paradise, a con's wet dream—no law—and this pussy doesn't realize how lucky he is. I'm not sure he's even happy to be out of prison."

"Well, he's good for carrying stuff and gathering wood for now. When we take the farm, he'll be our fetch boy."

The gravelly voice laughed, then hawked and spit. "Just so you know…the farmer's wife is Chuck's. We'll kill the rest."

The quiet man went back to being quiet.

Nate had gone to bed last night bone weary, and his back and leg muscles screamed all morning as he carried the heavy pack. Now rage surged through his veins, replenishing his strength. He was as angry for Susan and Beth as Brian, despite the fact they were dead and past hurting. His eyes were slits as he moved in for the kill. They came to murder his family; all thoughts of mercy or doubts about what he was about to do vanished. Pushing the safety off his rifle, he stalked closer.

All the colors of the forest became intense, every leaf and branch, every twig and blade of grass crisp and vivid in his eyes. Sounds funneled into his senses, not just his ears, but his very soul; he was a Ranger again, a Ranger at war.

Tracking them by sound, he came in from their left and caught them in an opening the size of a two-car garage. Their long guns hung from their shoulders, useless. All three saw him at the same time and froze, their faces ashen as they stared at the muzzle of his rifle. They had no idea who he was, but they saw hate on his face and death in his eyes. The one who had a handgun reached for it. Nate double tapped him, putting both bullets in his heart. He had the time since the other two would never get their long guns into action before he killed them.

The gravelly voiced man threw his arms up and yelled in a high-pitched scream, "I surrender!"

Nate put a bullet through the man's head and swung on the last man has he turned to run, shooting him twice in the back and out his chest. Blood and pieces of lung sprayed a palmetto frond. He fell, made a gurgling noise, and died.

A tinge of guilt hit Nate. He slammed a mental door in its face. *This isn't about justice or fairness; it's about them coming to kill my family.*

He tied their long guns on his pack. Picking up the pistol, he noticed *Property of Leon Co. Sheriff's Dept.* was engraved on the slide. He took the holster with its magazine pouch too.

In a hurry to get to Mel's cache and drugs, and then back to Brian, he didn't take time to search their pockets, but he did open their packs and dump everything out to quickly check for anything useful. He found the personal items of their past victims; mostly cash and jewelry, dirty clothing, and enough canned goods to last two or three days only. They had not figured out that cash is no longer king and gold is not going to fill your stomach. If they had any sense and knew of Mel's cache, they would not bother with the farm. Or was it all personal for Chuck Shingle?

With so few supplies, if they were waiting for Chuck Shingle and others, they expected them soon.

Nate ran. There was no time to waste. He had miles of rough country to cover, then the long trip back. As he ran, he thought about dumping the extra guns and emptying his pack, but pushed the thought aside and kept running.

The adrenaline surge faded and with it his energy, but he pushed himself and made it to the cave sooner than expected. His clothes were drenched in the thirty-six degree weather. He approached the entrance only after circling and checking to be certain no one was around or had been recently.

After worrying through all of Mel's security, he rushed into the cave and headed for a sealed plastic container marked MEDICAL SUPPLIES. It was the size of a small closet, and Nate hoped that meant it contained a virtual pharmaceutical warehouse. What he needed would have been difficult for Mel to buy, as it is normally restricted, but Mel had his ways of getting such things. He knew Mel even had weapons cached somewhere that were not exactly legal under federal and state law. When Mel started to mention what he had, Nate interrupted him and warned he did not want or need to know about anything illegal he had purchased and cached away for the end of the world. "You're a good man, and I hope you never need them or get into trouble," Nate told him. "And the fewer people know about it the better. Also, if I know about you doing something illegal, I could get dragged into any legal troubles of yours."

Nate found a shelf marked ANTIBIOTICS. Working feverously, he dumped everything out of his pack and left the killers' weapons by the pile on the floor. After taking everything he could find that could be an antibiotic, he searched for information on how to use them. He found what he was looking for on the same shelf. Handwritten across the cover was: ANTIBIOTIC DOSES; INDICATIONS; CONTRADICTIONS. Under that was: (When and how much to use and when not to.) He put the manual in his pack with the medication.

He dumped a handful of syringes in with the antibiotics and started to pick his pack up but stopped short. Searching the shelves again, this time for pain killer, he grabbed most of what was there and slipped the bottles in a side pocket of the pack. Sweat dripped from his face as he leaned over to secure the top flap. He slammed the pack on, slipping his left arm under a shoulder strap. After bolting and locking the cave door, he started back to Brian in a sprint.

Thirty minutes of plowing through the brush left him gasping. He pushed on at reckless speed. If Shingle and his fellow convicts were in the area, he might blunder into an ambush. Charging up a steep bluff, he reached the top out of breath and careened down the other side. A rock rolled under a foot and nearly sent him tumbling. Fear of rolling on the pack and breaking the bottles of medication that may save Brian's life went through his mind. He grabbed a sapling and managed to land on his butt. He slid the rest of the way down in that position.

At the bottom, he pushed up from the ground and stood gasping. *Slow down! You're going to break a leg. Then you will be no use to Brian.*

The thought of Brian lying in bed and those killers getting there before him spurred him on. He kept reminding himself what he heard the killers say about the others arriving later. Certainly it would not be today. But how could he be sure?

*   *   *

Brian slept peacefully; the book about home remedies lay open on his chest. He left the wounded leg uncovered because it felt hot. The towel under his wound was soaked through, staining the sheet under it. From the knee down, his leg felt numb, and the room smelled of something rancid and vulgar.

Many times he had thought there was nothing left to live for, he had no future. His father insisted he did, but he still saw little to live for and had wished himself dead several times. This morning he dozed off worrying about his father. What if he did die? His father would be alone in all this.

He dreamed he heard voices. Something, he did not know what, woke him. Opening his eyes, he looked around the dark room. Little afternoon sunlight found its way in through the shutters. The backdoor! He reached for the shotgun. The hammering told him it was not his father. All drowsiness vanished as his heart pounded. He thought he would never get enough air, his chest heaved.

Someone pounded on the shutter covering his bedroom window. It was an ax. Twice, the blade came through. Someone drove it through again and turned it in the wood, splintering a piece off.

Brian aimed the shotgun and waited. His heart beat against his chest.

The ax cut through again and a larger piece was levered away. Again, it drove through and was twisted. This time the handle broke, leaving the blade in the wood. Pounding came from the other end of the house.

There had been voices, but Brian could not hear what was said. Now he heard someone cussing. "You broke the handle. Idiot!"

"I'll get it open, Chuck. Just keep watch in case someone shows up before I get in."

"Just remember there's a chance they left the kids inside."

Brian saw a hand reach in and grope for the latch. He fired and the hand was removed at the wrist.

All hell broke loose. Bullets shattered through the shutter, splintering it further. Screaming and gunfire filled Brian's ears.

Brian slid himself to the foot of the bed to take refuge behind the steel plate Nate put up. His leg burned, but he hardly noticed. He jacked another round in the chamber and cowered behind the steel, wood splinters flying, some landing on his bed.

Screaming was all Brian heard above the ringing in his ears when the shooting stopped. Then the pounding on the front and back door started again. How many are there? Terror shook him to the bone. He knew now he wanted to live. How stupid was he to think of just giving his life away! No. He will fight for his life and never again think of giving up.

He fired through the open window and worked the slide, then rolled off onto the floor. A jolt of fire raced up his leg, and he fought back an urge to throw up. Another torrent of bullets came crashing into the room. Beside his bed was the

30/30. He grabbed it and crawled on his belly into the hallway with a gun in each hand.

The shooting stopped but the pounding on the doors didn't. They were handmade by his grandfather of solid oak. As sturdy as they were, they could not withstand the onslaught forever.

Outside, the man had stopped screaming. It seemed to Brian he was at the west end of the house because he moaned every few minutes .

Brian heard the front door splintering. They had gotten another ax, or perhaps a pickax, from the barn. There were plenty of tools for their choosing. He started to crawl for the living room. He would be there to greet him with buckshot.

A distant pop, followed by a *thwack*, came to Brian's ears. The man screamed again. More distant pops, and the man's screaming seemed to move to the front yard. As he ran, the popping continued, interspersed with more bullet impacts on his body.

A renewed torrent of gunfire roared from both sides of the house. They were shooting at someone in the woods. He knew that. But who? *The girl. She has the .22 rifle from those men at the river.*

He crawled back to the bed and pulled himself up. Leaving the shotgun in his lap, he shouldered his father's bolt-action and pushed the safety off. There was no time to get the shooting platform back in place.

A man bolted for the tree line on the west side of the field. Brian tried to get a shot but the man stumbled just before he pulled the trigger. A pop came just as he fell, and Brian knew the girl had hit him. The man jumped up and ran for the barn. Brian took too long to find him in the ten power scope. The range was too close. Brian realized he should have used his 30/30 instead.

There was more popping, and the man was hit at least once more before he got behind the barn. Brian could not see it from his angle, but he heard the impact and the man yell out, "Oh, shit!"

After five minutes of silence Brian, anxious, wondered what next. Catching movement in the tree line along the right side of the field, he snatched up the binoculars and scanned the shadows.

Brian's eyes rounded and he dropped the binoculars in his lap. Shouldering the bolt-action, he took careful aim. *Oh, hell!* He lowered the rifle and checked the range card.

Five hundred yards. Brian read the card showing holds for different ranges. *Minus 1.25 mils.*

It took Brian five seconds to find them again through the cope. They had walked another twenty yards, moving fast considering one of them was wounded. He estimated that meant he needed to aim one half a Mil Dot low with a six-hundred-yard zero. The shot left his ears ringing again. *I think I hit him.* Checking through the scope after chambering another round, he saw nothing more of the men.

Time ticked slowly by. Brian reloaded the shotgun and rifle, his hands shaking. He wondered if he had hit the man in the woods. *I hope the girl is okay. She sure saved my ass.* He glassed the western tree line, but saw no sign of her or anyone else. Stuffing a pillow between him and the headboard, he leaned back to rest his aching muscles. Pain shot down his leg. Looking down, he saw it was oozing fluid faster than before all the trouble started. Blood mixed with clear and yellow seepage and flowed onto the mattress. Brian worried about his father. *Did they kill him before they got here?* He wondered.

*   *   *

Nate ran as fast as he could, bulling through the brush and weaving through the trees. Fatigue had forced him to slow his screaming legs down, but the sound of gunfire coming from the direction of the farm slammed him into high gear. He even thought he heard a .22. Had Brian run the more powerful weapons dry and been reduced to the .22 rifle?

Coming up to the last half mile, he heard one more shot. He was certain it was his bolt-action. The silence that followed could not give him hope: it told him little.

Blood pounded through his head as he slowed to a walk. The closer he got to the farm, the more he forced himself to slow. As much as he wanted to keep running all-out, he knew better. His training would not allow him to rush into a firefight not knowing the strength and position of the enemy. He slowed still more, until he was in hunting mode.

Again, Nate found his senses on high intensity. A mosquito buzzed by his ear sounding like an airliner flying by. There was no wind, and the woods were listless death itself. He went into the highest stage of alert, stopping to stand and not moving again until he had searched every inch, every shadow, every tree, bush, or stump that could give refuge to waiting death. In less than seventy yards, he would see the back of the house. But he must see anyone waiting in ambush and put a bullet into him before he had a chance to do it to Nate. It should have taken an hour; he rushed it and in forty-two minutes he peered into the backyard from thick brush.

Nothing. Not a sound. No movement.

Nate saw the back door had been hacked into. He was relieved to see it was still intact. No one had entered through there at least, or anywhere else on the back side of the house.

Nate worked his way around, staying back in the brush, to the east end of the house.

Nothing. All the shutters seemed untouched. No one had entered here. He searched the near end of the barn, finding nothing. Slowly, he turned and searched the woods, his eyes straining to penetrate deep into the shadows. Still no movement. Nothing.

Turning back to the house, Nate saw red on the wall near the front corner. His heart skipped into high gear. Losing patience, he backed deeper into the brush, seeking shade and bullet-stopping cover. He yelled out at the top of his voice, "Brian, I'm coming in the usual way." Then he instantly dropped to his knees, half expecting to be answered with shots from the far woods.

Brian's voice came from the broken bedroom window. "Come on. I think they headed for the river."

New life shined in Nate's eyes. *He's alive!*

Chapter 9

Brian had a lot to say and words spewed out all at once. He made no sense until Nate told him to slow down.

"They were breaking in," Brian said. "One hacked a hole in the shutter and put his hand in. I shot it off with the shotgun. They shot through the shutter and I got behind the steel plate." He stopped for air. "Someone shot from the woods, sounded like a .22. Must've been the egg thief. She scared them off."

Nate looked him over while he talked. Brian's leg looked terrible, the bed was soaked with blood and other fluid from his wound, but otherwise he seemed unhurt. "It's cold in here." Sunlight slanted in the open window from the right. "This bed is filthy and littered with wood fragments. I'm taking you back to your bedroom."

Brian was still excited. "No way! Someone has to guard the window."

"Calm down. They're not crawling through that window today. When a dog runs yelping from a fight with his tail between his legs, he's not going to come back too quickly. Might try something early morning…three, four AM most likely…but I will be waiting." He pulled Brian to the edge of the bed.

Brian resisted. "Leave me here while you check on the girl. They shot at her a lot. She might be hurt."

Nate hesitated. "How far away do you think she was when she shot?"

Brian's eyes looked out the window, but Nate knew he was really looking through a thick fog of memory. "I think at least a hundred yards, probably more. The popping was real weak."

Nate relaxed. "I doubt they hit her then."

"But they might've. She was a long way off though. The bullets hitting the men were louder than the rifle. If she had a more powerful gun, she would have killed two of them."

Nate was preparing to lift him, but stood straight, his face showing pleasant surprise. "She hit two of them?"

"Yeah. The one I shot in the hand. She got him many times when he was against the house moaning. And another one who ran behind the barn cussing."

"Good," Nate said. "That means two are wounded, maybe dead. There should be two more. I will deal with them later."

Brian's face showed surprise. "How do you know how many?"

"I heard three more of the gang talking about killing us and taking the farm. They planned to camp by the river not far from Mel's and meet with four others later. Evidently your bunch."

"What did you do?"

"What do you think I did? They escaped from state prison. I heard one talking about killing a deputy. Afterwards, I ran to Mel's, got the drugs, and ran back here. Heard the last of the shooting and snuck up ready for a fight. Only the fight was already over."

He pulled Brian closer and lifted him.

Brian protested. "No. You got to check on the girl first. I owe her."

Nate carried him down the hall. "She's proven to be no fool. I guarantee you she was behind cover and concealment before she fired the first shot. Those killers were firing blind into the woods. You're right about owing her—both of us."

It took Nate two hours to clean Brian up, read the information in Mel's drug manual, give him an injection of the proper dosage, and get him to stop talking about the events of the afternoon long enough to eat. The drug was out-of-date, but the manual said it could still be used if it had not turned dark. This information was a notation of Mel's. He prayed Mel was right. If Brian's leg did not appear much worse, Nate would never have taken the chance.

"If your leg is bothering you too much to sleep, you might as well take one of the pills." Nate felt Brian's leg to see how hot it was and sat back in his chair. "We have plenty of painkillers now. I grabbed all Mel had when I was there."

Brian was still nervous. "We can't sleep, they'll come back tonight."

"If they do it'll be hours from now. And I was talking about you sleeping, not me. You can stand guard tomorrow."

"I would rather be awake when they come."

Nate laughed. "That seems reasonable. But they may not come back tonight or tomorrow. How long do you think you can go without sleep?"

Brian sighed with frustration and pain. "I don't see anything funny." He crossed his arms on his chest and looked away.

Nate smiled. "I'm just glad you don't have any more holes in you. Now that we have the drugs, you have a good chance."

"I hope the drugs work." Brian looked at his father. "I changed my mind about wanting to die."

Nate stopped rubbing his aching calf muscles and looked up from the chair. "You don't want to leave me anymore?"

"I never said that." Brian's voice was tinged with anger.

"Result would be the same."

Brian closed his eyes and swallowed. He said nothing.

Nate saw the change on his face. "After all that's happened, here we are in one piece and at ninety-eight point six degrees. I am grateful."

Brian opened his eyes and looked up at the ceiling. "So am I."

Every muscle in Nate's body ached, but as he sat there looking at his son, all the pain and weariness inside washed away. But he knew it would return. *This hell is just beginning, and Brian's leg isn't well yet.*

*   *   *

"It's time for another injection." Nate hated waking Brian, but there was no choice. He shook him until he stirred.

Brian opened his eyes slightly. They were slits and unfocused as he looked at his father in the dim glow of the lamp, its wick turned down to reduce the light it produced. Then they opened wide, alarm on his face. He started to rise as if he were going to jump out of bed.

"Hold on! Just lie back. Everything is okay. I have to give you another shot."

Brian relaxed, settling back and pulling his blanket up to his chin. "It's cold."

"Yep. And so is your leg." Nate grabbed the sleeping bag nearby and spread it over Brian, but leaving his lower leg uncovered. "At least it's not as hot as it was four hours ago. That's all the difference I can see so far, but it's way too soon to expect much. It's a good sign though."

"Have they been sneaking around?" Brian asked.

"Can't see with the shutters closed. No way to know how serious Chuck Shingle and his gang are about killing us and taking the farm. They may have left, or they may be out there now planning and waiting."

"You know one of the bastards?"

Nate suddenly looked weary. "Had a run-in with him when I was in high school. He spent some time in jail over it. That was nothing new for him, nor was it his last. He finally got sentenced to life for murder. They should have allowed the human race to take a dump by executing him. But that's past history. He evidently talked his bunch into coming here when they escaped from state prison. He hates me—and your mother."

"Mom? The piece of shit!"

"Evidently they haven't bothered to case the place and find the graves, so they don't know she's gone."

"So they don't know how many guns are waiting for them."

"Yes," Nate said. "There are a few things in our favor: They don't know you're bedridden, Susan is gone, or how many are in here. They also do not know yet I killed the other three. It's likely they're heading upriver to join up with them before they try anything again. The real game changer is the girl out there. Someone in the woods who can shoot makes them nervous. It's too risky for them to just come back and try their stunt again until they know more about what they have taken on. Chuck's little maggots are giving him grief about making us look easy, I can assure you of that. He's probably got a mutiny on his hands."

"And some deserters."

"Yep. Two are wounded. And—"

"Maybe three," Brian said. "I'm sure I got one with that last shot. Might be dead."

"The one you crippled is worthless, maybe dead. In fact most likely. You say she hit him too. Both he and the other she hit multiple times are either dead or worthless."

"She hit them both all right, I heard it."

"Well," Nate said, "those little bullets were nearly spent, but they went deep enough to reach organs and major blood vessels. Depends on where she hit them. Anyway, they're going to die, or already have."

"Good."

"Good for us. Dead convicts can't hurt us."

"Even so, they wanted to hurt my mother. They can go to hell."

"They will…if the preachers know what they're talking about. You should cool off though. We need to keep level heads on our shoulders to get through this."

Nate cleaned Brian's leg with alcohol and gave him an injection.

Brian showed no reaction when Nate pushed the needle in. "That girl is in danger. You know it. They might be hunting her now. We can't just stay here and let them kill her. I can walk."

Nate tried to search his son's soul. His little boy was dying, and a man was taking his place. He did not know how to feel about it. He did know it was too soon. "I can't see them doing what I couldn't do."

"What?" Brian seemed confused.

"They will never lay eyes on her. If they hunt her, they're pissing in the wind. I was more surprised when I learned she was a girl, and so young, than you were. She's that good. Of course I didn't know she wasn't armed when I hunted her. I could have taken more chances and maybe at least gotten a look at her. Now she *is* armed, and they know it. They're stupid, but they know she can shoot, and they have proof how dangerous she can be. No, they are not in a hurry to tangle with her or us tonight."

"They don't know she's just some girl we don't know either; probably think she's part of the family, maybe you or your son."

"True," Nate said. "They are more in the dark about what they're up against than we are. That's good. Makes them nervous."

"Think they might give up and leave?"

"Possible some will. Chuckey's not going to live over this though, no matter what happens he's a dead SOB. His feud with me and my family ends soon. If he runs, I will hunt him down."

"Now you're the one who should cool off."

"Oh, the only thing about what I have planned for him that's hot is the lead; the rest will be served cold."

"Revenge."

"I've had enough of Chuckey, Brian. You and I have plenty of other things to worry about without him in this world." He stood. "Get some sleep. I will need you to stay awake tomorrow while I rest. It will be a few more hours before they come. If they come tonight."

*　　　*　　　*

It was just one shot. Wood splinters landed on Brian and the sleeping bag. Nate ran into the room and kept Brian down. "Just stay where you are. They can't shoot through the block walls with the rock facing. Stay down, below the window."

"Give me the shotgun," Brian said. "They'll come through the windows."

The night returned to silence.

Nate put his finger to his lips. He listened.

Nothing.

Brian gripped the shotgun, barrel slanting up towards the broken glass and closed shutters. Thirty minutes later another shot came through a window on the other side of the house.

Nate bent down to Brian's ear. "They're harassing us so we can't get any sleep tonight. Just try to rest. I'm here. This is my watch. Yours will start at sunrise."

Thirty more minutes of silence ended with another shot. It was followed in less than two seconds by the pop of a .22, which in turn, was followed by a scream.

A man yelled, "Oh, fuck!" The girl had found him by his muzzle flash.

Nate ran to the other end of the house. "Hurt did it? If you don't want more, you need to pack up and cut your losses before they grow."

"You're dead. You son of a bitch!" The voice came from trees not far from the house.

Nate knew the voice.

"No Chuckey, I'm feeling just fine. Many of *your* bunch aren't doing so well though." Chuck Shingle hated being called Chuckey and Nate knew it. "Don't bother looking for the three upriver; they died yesterday...after telling us your plans. We were waiting for you."

"Chuck!" A voice came from out of the dark woods. "You son of a bitch! Look what you've talked us into. Of all the farms we *could* have taken." It was the man who had just felt the sting of the girl's rifle. "You can have this shit. I'm gone. I've already lost a finger, that's enough."

Shingle's voice reverberated with rage. "I'm telling you, you gutless bastard, there's enough food here to live well for a year."

A barrage of shots came through the back door.

Nate dropped to his belly, rifle in hand.

"Dad!"

Nate yelled down the hall, "Stay where you are and keep quiet."

The barrage ceased.

"You're going to run out of ammo, Chuckey," Nate yelled. "We've got thousands of rounds, how about you?"

"Yeah," Shingle yelled back, "that's why the sniper is using a .22."

"My neighbor just happened to be hunting squirrels when you started this party. Good shot though, isn't he? I met him in Ranger School."

Silence.

"Chuckey, as is your habit, you didn't think this through. The house is rock-covered block with a metal roof. The only thing you can do is burn the barn, and what good will that do you? We have plenty of water and food. Play the waiting game and you lose, asshole."

Silence.

"The three we killed had little food and I doubt you do either. You're going to get hungry trying to wait us out, Chuckey."

Another barrage of shots came through the door.

Nate tried to determine the angle the shots were coming from, got on his knees and fired in a horizontal spray, spaced to cover a sector that left no man-sized holes in it. He dropped to the floor and rolled across the room.

Silence again.

Nate slipped a fresh twenty round magazine in the M14.

"Chuckey, you still there?"

Silence.

Nate laughed as loud and strong as he could. He did not feel like laughing, but he hoped it would burn Chuck Shingle's ears. Shingle had a temper, and the surest way to make him mad was to hurt his ego.

"Hey, Chuckey, you know what the coach always said: You can take the white trash boy out of White Trash Hollow, but you can't take the white trash out of the boy. Everyone knew he was talking about you."

When there was no gunfire or verbal assault, Nate knew Shingle was either dead or no longer within hearing. Shingle did not have much self-control, just one reason he had spent so much time behind bars.

Perhaps Nate hit him or at least came close enough to scare him into backing off for a while. He hoped he was lying out there dead. But there was no way to be sure until daylight.

After an hour, Nate rushed past the back door and went down the hall, keeping low for safety. Entering Brian's room, he found him awake, the shotgun in his hands, pointed loosely at the shuttered window.

"You need to sleep," Nate said. "This is still my watch."

Brian gave him a look that said it all. "You're joking. Sleep? They're shooting at us."

"Not now."

Brian rubbed his leg. "They were, and will again anytime."

"You're going to wish you had slept while you had the chance. Morning will be your watch from sunrise till ten."

"You're going to need more sleep than that, Dad."

"I'll be fine as long as I get a few hours. In Ranger school we went months on an average of one hour of rest out of twenty-four."

"Bull!"

"We were on our feet twenty out of twenty-four and went without food on some days. Some guys hallucinate from physical exhaustion and lack of sleep. If they can't get a grip, they wash out. We did get a night's sleep before we HALOed—high altitude, low opening— into Eglin for the swamp segment of the course."

Brian looked at his father with tired eyes. "Why did they let you sleep that one time before you jumped?"

"Too dangerous to HALO jump while that tired. How likely is it for soldiers to have to jump after months of combat with no rest in the real world? When soldiers jump into combat, they're usually fresh; it's the beginning of their involvement in a battle."

"I didn't know. You never told me. Never said anything about how you got wounded either."

Nate shrugged his shoulders. "Boring stuff. What we've been through lately overshadows my short Army career. It would put you to sleep."

"I need something to put me to sleep."

"How about I make us a sandwich?" Nate stood and then stepped aside so he could not be shot through the shutters. "Neither of us ate anything in many hours."

"Okay, but they may be going after the girl or up to something else."

"They *may* be doing a lot of things."

"Yeah, that's what I said, smart aleck." Brian smiled.

"They may be trying to hot-wire the truck or tractor. They're wasting time. I disabled them a few days back by removing a few parts."

"Oh."

"They may be looking for gas or diesel in the barn, they won't find any. I hid what little we had by burying it in the chicken feed bin. They may be trying to siphon some out of the truck and tractor to burn us out with, the tanks are empty."

"You drained them." Brian had a smirk on his face.

"Yep."

"Like I said you're a smart aleck." Brian's smirk was still there.

Nate looked at his watch. "It's early, but I might as well give you a shot now during this lull in the action."

The smile on Brian's face vanished.

Chapter 10

As the sun rose, Brian remained asleep. Nate could not bring himself to wake him. *Let him sleep. His leg's getting better now. Thank God and Mel's drugs.*

Every inch of Nate's body screamed for rest. *I'm damn sure not as young as I was in my Army days, but I have one more long battle left in me.* He referred to raising Brian, not just the current troubles. *I better; a father's contract with his children is never voided.*

Nate looked through bullet holes in a living room window shutter. Fog hung low, just above the warm earth. A dip in the pasture held a cloud of fog denser than the rest, like a bowl of whipped cream. The fog there was so thick he could see only a hint of the trees behind. Mist drifted up from the river that was too low in the valley to see from the house. The world was new again, reborn and one hour old, still wet behind the ears, as Nate's father used to say of the morning dew.

Somewhere in that fog, and the woods it shrouded, predators waited for him or Brian or the girl to make a fatal mistake. After he got some rest, he would go out there and hunt them down.

Nate looked to his right. A cowling on the tractor was pulled aside. Nate knew they had been at the pickup too. Chuck Shingle must have convinced them to stay and fight. No, the convicts had not given up and gone looking for easier prey. They were out there. They wanted his life and Brian's and the girl's.

"No. Hell no."

Nate gripped his rifle; it weighed a ton to his weary arms. Hate's talons tightened around his heart, leaving his chest tight. *Last night was your hunt; tonight is mine.*

If not for the danger to the girl, he could set traps. He knew a dozen ways to maim, even kill a man with booby traps. He was also worried about her out there while he hunted them in the dark. It was one reason he stayed in the house. That and Brian needing injections. He could shoot her or her him. Fratricide takes its toll in every war. When seconds mean life or death, mistakes will be made. Pull the trigger too late, you're dead, too soon, and you may kill a friend. The fog now beginning to lift will return with nightfall and with it the fog of war.

*   *   *

Brian listened for any sound that would warn him of danger. It was all he could do since all the windows were shuttered and he could not see out. Even the shutter the man hacked up with an ax was replaced by his father. Nate turned the steel plate on end so it would be tall enough, placing it against the window and then pushing a dresser up against it. His father warned him not to look out through the holes in the shutters and to stay away from the windows altogether. "Stay low and away from the windows and doors," Nate said. "Just listen. Hear anything outside, wake me."

But he was standing on his good leg and not staying low like his father told him. He felt the need to walk a little, get some blood flowing in his legs.

His father was asleep, not in bed, but on the living room floor. He said he could get into action quicker, and it was safer. He laid there with his rifle across his chest, still in his boots, his load-bearing harness beside him. Brian was not fully convinced he told him the total truth. Did he feel safer sleeping on the ground because that is where he had slept when he was fighting for the country?

A midday sun beat down strong, but Brian shivered in the cold, keeping a blanket wrapped around him. His leg too, was cold. His father told him that meant the infection was fading. He hoped so. He thought he felt better than yesterday. It was difficult to say for sure though. He was just too tired to tell.

Thwack!

Splinters from a living room window shutter flew across the room, and a bullet lodged in the back of a couch, stuffing exploded in the air like smoke.

"Hit the floor!" Nate's words were unnecessary. Brian was already dropping to his knees, grimacing from the pain of his wound. Then he rolled on his side next to the front wall.

They lay there on the living room hardwood floor, looking at each other. For some reason Brian started laughing. He found the scene hilarious.

Nate's face showed puzzlement for a second. Then he too, started to laugh. "You crazy kid. Is this really funny?"

"I guess not. For some reason it seems funny."

Another round came in through the same window, this one putting a hole in the floor just behind Nate. He grabbed his harness with extra magazines and fast-crawled over to the wall not far from Brian. "He must be shooting from a tree. It's the only way the bullets could be coming at that angle."

"The bastard almost got you," Brian said. "I wish Grandpa had put steel shutters in."

"He was thinking of hurricanes, not bullets."

"I didn't mean to laugh at you nearly getting shot."

Nate's eyes flashed to his son. "You laughed before that."

"I don't know why I thought it was funny. Us lying on the floor I guess."

"You're giddy from lack of sleep. We both are. Stay here. I'm getting the bolt-action and binocs. If he's in a tree, I'll find him and take him out."

"He's just shooting blind like last night."

"Yeah," Nate said, "but they're trying to get the bullets to hit lower where they know we'll be."

"If he's in a tree on the other side of the field, it must be a tall one."

Another bullet crashed in, this one through the kitchen window.

Nate looked around the room. "Get over there in the corner. Someone might shoot through the back door."

Brian crawled to where he was told. "How are you going to see without opening a shutter and exposing yourself?"

"That steel plate is not tall enough to cover the top few inches of the window. I think I can sit on the shooting platform and shoot. If he's in a tall tree, he'll be an easy shot."

Thwack!

A bullet came through the front door.

Nate crawled down the hall. He came back in a few minutes and tossed one of the electronic ear protectors to Brian. Then he started back to the bedroom.

Brian turned the knob and put them on. He settled down in the corner with the shotgun trained on a back window.

It did not take Nate long to find him with the binoculars. He was already climbing down. Nate quickly shouldered the rifle and aimed. He started the squeeze. Before the sear released, the man jumped the rest of the way, disappearing in brush. "Shit!" He took his finger off the trigger. Nate derided himself for taking too long to think of the idea and too long to execute it.

Brian heard. "What?"

Nate turned the volume on his shooting muffs higher. "I found him, but he was already climbing down and jumped the rest of the way just before I shot."

"He might climb another."

"Yeah, to get a different angle. I want you to come in here. Stay low."

Brian looked up at his father as he sat on the floor. "What?"

"Open the range box and get our shooting glasses out. There are wood splinters and bullet fragments flying. I should have thought of that a long time ago."

Brian handed him shooting glasses and put the others on. "You can't think of everything."

"Get back down." Nate glassed the tree line. "We *must* think of everything. The price of a mistake is too high."

"Those stupid crooks can't stand in your shadow. You've beat them at every turn. We'll make it."

Nate looked down at Brian. His eyes changed from worry and anger directed at the convicts to a softer tone. He set the rifle down and got off the platform.

Grabbing the mattress, he turned the dirty side down and put it on the floor beside the bed. "You're not well yet. You need to rest."

"I'm better now."

Nate pointed. "Lie down. It's time for another injection anyway. I will clean the wound again too."

"I told you I'm better. They're shooting at us! And you stop for this?"

"We probably have only one chance to get you well, Nate said, "I don't want you getting worse again."

"But—"

"The real fight is tonight, Brian. And that one is all mine. Your fight is getting well and not collecting anymore bullet holes."

Brian rested on the mattress while Nate examined the wound. "It's definitely not as red or swollen. The bandage was not soaked so much with drainage either." He wiped the wound with antibiotic soaked gauze.

"I told you I'm getting better. The drug is working." Brian flinched when Nate rubbed too hard.

"I have to keep giving you the injections until the infection is completely gone. If it comes back it will be more resistant to the drug."

A bullet ricocheted off something in the kitchen, followed by a rifle report that sounded closer than the last shots.

Nate scrambled up on the platform and shouldered the rifle. Searching with bare eyes, he found the man climbing down a tall pine only one hundred yards away. He aimed four and one half Mil Dots low and fired. The impact was hard to miss, blood sprayed as the bullet exited his torso. He bounced when he landed at the foot of the tree. There was no movement. Nate, worked the bolt, took careful aim, and put another bullet through his chest to be sure. Quickly, he chambered a fresh round.

"Get him?" Brian asked.

"He's dead. Couldn't miss at that range." Nate had the binoculars to his eyes.

"Is it Chuckey?"

"No. Chuckey has a deformed face. This guy is ugly but not Chuckey."

Brian looked disappointed. "I guess I didn't hit that one I shot at back in the trees just before you got here."

Nate looked through the binoculars at the dead man again. "It's the one our woodsman friend, uh…woodsgirl…shot last night. He has a rag on his hand."

"He just hasn't had much luck lately," Brian replied dryly. "First his finger, now his head."

Nate chuckled under his breath, despite their predicament. "He should have left last night. Chuckey always could talk idiots into doing foolish things, sometimes even girls. He has a couple kids somewhere, or did. The taxpayers were raising them. Who knows now if they're still alive, with the sickness."

"What happened to Chuckey's face?" Brian asked. "Car accident?"

"Baseball bat."

"Wow. Who did it?"

"Me," Nate said. "Don't talk so much. We need to be able to hear them coming up."

"You're talking. You just don't want to tell me what happened. Why does he hate Mom?"

Nate smiled. "They're shooting at us, and you want to talk?"

Brian rolled his eyes. "Funny."

"Why don't you sleep?"

"You're the one who is supposed to be sleeping. This is my watch."

"Taking one of them out is worth losing sleep. Our odds just got better."

"You have something planned for tonight," Brian said, "so you should sleep now."

"It's still early. There is plenty of time for me to sleep. I'm hoping to get a shot at Chuckey. He might try to collect the dead man's rifle and ammo. They are probably running low on ammo by now."

Brian sat up on the mattress. "Oh, that's what you're up to."

"He's not likely to be *that* stupid, but I can hope."

"How many does that leave?" Brian looked up at his father, rubbing his leg. "And where is the girl?"

Nate lowered the binoculars, his eyes looking inward. "Near as I can tell, there is one left besides Chuckey. At least one left who has not had his hand shot off. The one you shot can't be of any use. If he's still alive. Then she added to his troubles by using that .22 rifle on him. No, he's not one of them shooting at us. The other one she pumped .22s into may be dead or not, but he's not likely to be a threat either. Basically, Chuckey is alone." Nate looked down at Brian. "You have as good an answer to your last question as me."

"I hope she's okay," Brian said. "She's helped us a lot and put herself in danger."

"I second that. I'll go further and hope she has left the area for now. She has been a godsend, but it would be safer for me tonight if she were not out there. I don't want to worry about her shooting me in the dark. And I don't want to get killed because I hesitated to avoid shooting her."

Brian grimaced when he moved his leg. "I think you should just stay in the house. It's worked so far. Let him wander around out there in the cold while we stay warm, or at least warmer, inside."

"I'm afraid Chuckey will leave now that his little army has been whittled down. If that happens, he may come back when our guard is down. When there was law and society, I had to tolerate him, though he was a danger to my family. Now I want Chucky out of my life permanently. He's trash, a parasite, and nothing but a source of misery."

"You mean out of the world."

"Same thing."

"Not quite, Dad, but I agree with you. I just don't see any point in you going out there when you're safer in the house."

"He will get away," Nate said, "that's the point. He may be putting miles between us now. This has been going on since I was about four years older than you. It ends tonight." Nate stiffened. "Quiet. There's movement in the woods by that tree." He glassed the area. "Somebody back there crawling, real slow. Can't see if it's Chuckey." Nate shouldered the rifle, looking through the ten power scope. "I'll be damned!"

Brian grabbed the shotgun and sat up. "What?"

"Shh, I'm busy." Nate searched with the binoculars again. This time he was searching the tree line on the other side of the field. He kept the rifle in his right hand, shouldered with muzzle down, bipod resting on the platform, ready for quick use. He could drop the binoculars and raise the rifle in a second.

Several minutes went by.

"Dad, will you please tell me what the hell is going on?"

"Quiet. She's exposed. I'm covering the other tree line in case Chuckey's over there and tries to take a shot at her."

Brian's eyes grew large. "The girl?"

"There's only one I know of." Nate laughed out loud.

"What?"

The girl was lying next to the body, searching his pockets. She pulled out a few rifle rounds and stuffed them in her jeans.

"She waved at us. She knows I can see her. I just hope Chuckey can't." He trained the binoculars back on the tree line where danger lurked.

"What does she look like?"

Nate snickered and trained the binoculars back on her. "She's got his rifle and ammo and crawling deeper into the woods now. I can't see her anymore. She's safe."

He searched the other tree line again out of hope for a shot at Chuck Shingle.

Brian got up and stood on his good leg. When he tried to get on the platform, Nate noticed the movement. He jerked the binoculars down and turned to look at Brian. "Hey! Get back on that mattress. I have not bandaged your leg yet. You'll get it dirty. You've seen girls before. What's wrong with you?"

Brian's face turned red. "I just wanted to see who saved my life." He lay back down, crossing his arms on his chest, obviously in a huff.

Nate looked at Brian, a twinkle in his eye. "She's too old for you anyway." He smiled. "And ugly to boot. I guess you can't go by a girl's voice in the dark." He laughed at Brian's

Chapter 11

"Don't go out there, Dad."

"The cow's got to be fed and milked," Nate said. "I'll circle around and make sure Chuckey's not out there first. That will take some time, so don't worry if I'm not back in a few hours. Then I'll feed the chickens, collect the eggs, and take care of the cow. We also need some water in here."

Brian's eyes knitted. "We're not even going to be able to keep the cow at Mel's. You said we'll have to butcher it for meat."

"Yes, but right now it's standing in its own crap and hungry and its udder is full."

"Okay." Brian's voice told Nate he was reluctant to give in, but knew Nate was right: It is wrong to neglect their livestock.

"We'll have eggs for supper."

"Of course." Brian rolled his eyes. "What else? Then what? It's almost over now, why push it?"

"I'll go hunting while you stay here."

"Dad…"

"What? Do you want that bastard out there waiting for a chance to kill us? We have to move; we will be vulnerable while packing all our stuff. We will be sitting ducks on the river in that water tank."

Brian's breathing increased with anguish. "I hope he has headed for the next county."

"Maybe he has. The trouble is he keeps coming back. He even escaped from a life sentence. And what does he do? He gathers a gang of thugs and heads for us. He's got to die, Brian. With no law now, he's got a free hand. How many average people could have stopped him like we did? Most people are peaceful and can't handle raw violence and savagery. He is a wolf and they're sheep. He's a danger to everyone."

Brian blinked and turned away. "Be careful."

"I will," Nate said. "Get the shotgun and be ready to do like we planned." He put his left hand on Brian's shoulder.

His rifle was in his right. "After the door is barred, get off your leg until I return. You're still not well."

"Okay."

"I know this has been hard on you. You've grown inside many years in the last few months. I'm sorry. A boy should be allowed to be a boy until it's time to be a man. It's not fair, none of this is, but I have done the best I could, I always will."

"I know," Brian said. "It's not your fault. I was just thinking when you said most people are peaceful that we used to be peaceful too."

"Things are not the same. You know we still do not hurt good people."

Brian's face changed. "I know, but we're still killing *people*."

"Yes we are. And it's good we haven't forgotten that and never will."

"But I laughed at the one guy getting shot."

"I did too. Soldiers do things like that in war sometimes. It relieves the tension. They go home and are good people who served their country and suffered for others. Brian, you are a good person. You have done nothing to be ashamed of. They came to kill us. We defended ourselves. Whether we laugh or cry about it makes no difference, the facts are the same. *They* caused this to happen. Don't let it eat you up."

"I know, but I laughed."

Nate's eyes softened. "Damn it, Brian, none of this is your fault. If there is any fault on our side—and I say there isn't—it's mine, all mine. I am your father and you did what I told you, not to mention you only defended yourself, so any fault is mine. Please don't hurt over this, you've been through more than enough already."

Nate unlocked the door and removed the bar, making as little noise as possible. Brian stood against the wall beside the door, shotgun in one hand, the steel bar in the other. It was heavy, but he managed with one arm. Nate swung the door open and rolled out onto the back porch which was little more than a concrete slab. He reached up and pushed the door closed behind him.

As he had been told, Brian waited five seconds. When there was no gunfire, he slid the bar in place. He leaned against the wall, blinking tears. "Be careful Dad."

It was cold but not so much as the night before. With not a breath of wind, the woods were petrified and deathly silent. There were no insect sounds. Too cold. Nate slipped in among the trees and immediately sought out the shadows. The sound of the frozen ground crunching under his boots forced him to walk slow, easing his weight onto his forward foot. Silence and shadow were life, he meant to live.

In half an hour he was deep into the dark and obscurity of the moonless forest night. He allowed himself to sink silently into the pitch black of his battleground.

A wide arc around the east side of the farm and field was clean of Chuck Shingle, the girl, or any other human. An hour and a half of careful stepping, standing, listening, and looking left him certain of that. He moved on, in a slow, disciplined way, one step a minute, until he had come down to the river swamp.

Here, in the swamp, darkness was refined and concentrated, transformed into something altogether different that needed a new word to describe it, for 'dark' was far too weak. He knew it well. The darkness of the swamp that is, this being his home. And he had trained in Panama just after Ranger School and fought in a South American jungle just before he left the Army. So he knew too the slow rush of the jungle death hunt, a constant and steady fear that often exploded into a fast and deadly skirmish—over so soon, but leaving the jungle floor littered with mangled dead and dying. In the crucible of war, necessity, the will to live, forced him to develop a sense beyond seeing, hearing, touching, smelling, and tasting that had kept him alive and sent many of other races and governments to their death. But tonight not one lumen managed to filter through the swamp canopy above, and his eyes were nearly useless. He knew what he was doing when he entered, walked willingly, but only because it was necessary, into hell.

Downward to the river: that was his compass. Some hundred yards from the watery bottom, he smelled death. Vectoring in, his nose leading him, he found Brian's handless housebreaker. He lay in a rare cool dappling of starlight, and Nate could just see etchings of agony on his death face. It was too cold for insects, and there were no ants. *Thank God it was you and not my son, you son of a bitch.*

When he reached water's edge, he turned to the west and let the toes of his boots warn him of cypress knees and roots and rooted-out holes left by wild hogs. The minutes floated by in a sluggish current, and time slowed until one step was an eternity, one heartbeat an hour. By the time he came out of the trees onto the bluff above the river and below his farm, the transmigration was complete. What emerged, one slow inch by slow inch, from the deep dark of treed swamp into the shallow dark of open starry sky was not what entered, sank into the other side. Brian would not have recognized this predator.

Nate low-crawled for the tree line. It was too open there to stand and walk, even in the moonless dark. Down at water's edge where the bluff dropped shear to the riverbank, a hog snorted when it caught the smell of danger above and rushed downriver into the swamp on the western side of the farm. Nate continued on until he was in the shadows again. Standing, he waited many minutes to allow not just his eyes to adjust, but all other senses. The hog's fright could have alerted anyone nearby, so he waited longer, standing in shadow, listening. Then he resumed the hunt, this time up the slope and on the other side of the field, away from the river.

Again, Nate smelled death. He knew before he found the body it would be the girl's kill. It was no more than a presence in the dark and the source of a stench. A hog had torn into it and left it mutilated. Once it had been a man of sorts, of a plebian kind anyway: a creature with a diseased soul. The divide separating Nate, the predator, from what the man was before he was turned into a lump of rotting flesh was narrow, but that divide made all the difference. Nate's killer instinct was under the control of a soul determined to never harm an innocent. The dead man had deliberately singled out the most innocent to prey on until he made the fatal mistake of coming to this farm.

Up the slope, Nate inched his way. Not far from the one he shot out of the tree, that feeling from an earlier time in his life came racing back: He felt the presence of another predator. Nate never talked of this ability with anyone but those who had been in combat, and then, only those who were members of recon or sniper teams. Always, he had let others bring up the subject, it being such a difficult thing to believe unless you had experienced it yourself. But once it was broached, he admitted that he too, could sense when he was being hunted and knew when a rifle was aimed at him. No one he had ever talked to about it, almost always at a bar where soldiers gathered, had an explanation better than or even as good as his own. But it was real, that, all who had experienced it agreed. Tonight, he knew he was being hunted and had been since he first neared the tree sniper's body.

The girl? He did not know, but he or she was in the dark, waiting.

He started deeper into the trees, intending to kill whoever it was; it could be Chuck Shingle. *It could be the girl.* He stopped and waited. Decision made, he swung around, in his disciplined way, making sure he swung wide and far. Then he inched upslope and around to the left, around the back of the house, always in the trees, the shadows, and then further around to the barn, the last in the open.

Nate passed the chicken coop. He fed the cow and shoveled her stall clean while she chewed, tied to a post outside the stall. He fed the chickens. They would not leave their nests or eat until morning, but the feed was there for them. Then he gathered eggs before going to the pump. He needed water. There was soap in the barn to clean the cow and the milk pail before milking her, but the pump was their only source of water since the power went out.

He watered the hens and the cow, which drank so much he was forced to go for another pail for her and one for cleaning.

An hour later, Nate spoke up from the woods behind the house. "Brian, I'm coming in."

Nate heard the bar slide. He rushed to the door and dropped to the concrete slab of a porch, pulling it open while on his knees, then rolling in, turning on his back, pulling it closed behind him.

Standing in the dark by the door, Brian slid the bar in place, the shotgun in his right hand. "What took so long?"

Nate walked into the kitchen and took a pail off the table. "I've got eggs out there and a pail of milk. First, I'll fill this with water while you stand guard."

Brian lit a lamp. When he turned and looked at Nate, what he saw chilled him. He did not see his father. He saw cold death in a strange creature's eyes. This was from the side. The warm glow of the kerosene lamp painting his father's profile did nothing to dull the chill of Brian's blood. When Nate moved his head, his eyes swung and aimed at him. They were double barrels on a turret of a head. Brian recoiled, pulled back.

"Put that lamp out," Nate said. "We both need our night vision."

Brian did not move.

Nate did not understand what was wrong with him. There was fear in Brian's eyes. He swung around with his rifle, expecting to see Chuck Shingle holding a gun to his back. Turning back to Brian, he asked, "What are you afraid of?"

Brian swallowed. "Nothing."

There was a sudden softening of Nate's eyes. "It's just your dad, Brian. I'm...not mad at you, nor am I going to hurt you. I just spent many hours out there in the dark hunting an animal that dwarfs any other predator on this planet in killing ability. That's going to do something to you, no matter what kind of person you are." He smiled. "By the time I'm through cooking those eggs, I won't look so mean. Now kill that light."

"Okay."

They stood in the dark until Nate said, "I'm going to open the kitchen window shutter so you can watch the right side, nearest the woods. Stay back from the window and just look that way. I'll take care of the other side." Brian walked closer to him. Nate laid his left hand on Brian's shoulder. "Listen to me now. If someone shoots from behind the tractor or from the woods, you will see the muzzle flash. Chuckey is right-handed, so shoot to the right of the flash about six inches. At that range the buckshot pattern will have spread so much it won't matter if you're off a little. The problem is there will be holes in the pattern. That can't be helped. Just shoot to the right once and duck down below the window. You got that? Once, no more."

Brian nodded in the dark. "Okay. But it will hit the tractor."

"We will deal with that if it happens. Just one shot and then duck and stay down. You understand?"

"Yes."

Nate's voice sounded adamant. "Pump another shell in *after* you duck, not before."

"Right."

Nate opened the window shutters and looked out into the dark. He still could not see much, so they stood there several more minutes.

"The door will be left open so I can rush back in." He pulled Brian to the left a little. "Do not move from this spot. If you shoot, drop to the floor and stay there."

"Okay."

They both turned on their hearing protection and put them on. Nate opened the front door.

Surrounded by dark, there was little he could do to stop anyone from shooting him as he walked to the pump, so he walked as if there was no danger at all. When he had the pail nearly full, he carried it back into the house, set it down just to the side of the doorway, and, with rifle in hand, he ran to the barn.

A few seconds later, Nate headed across the yard and into the house with a pail in each hand, spilling some of the milk.

He set the pails down and had the door closed and barred in less than three seconds. All this time, he had his rifle in his right hand.

Brian released a lung full of nervous air.

Nate closed the kitchen window shutter. Turning in the dark to Brian, he said, "Relax. It's over for tonight." He rubbed his hands together. "I'm hungry. Now you can light that lamp."

"Damn, Dad."

"What? Aren't you hungry?"

"Yeah. But you act like it was nothing."

"It was. Nothing happened, so it *was* nothing. I was just out there for hours earlier tonight."

"But you weren't so much a sitting duck."

Nate had an amused look on his face, but Brian could not see it in the dark. "I wasn't out there just going for a walk. I was checking to make sure no one was out there waiting in the woods. I circled the entire farm. All I found was a hog down by the river and the man you shot and the one the girl shot. The hog was alive but the others were ripe, despite the cool weather."

Brian started to chuckle but caught himself. "We shouldn't laugh. I'm glad they can't hurt us though."

"Well, it's over for now, except for Chuckey, so light that lamp and let's eat."

"I'm trying to find a match." Brian fumbled in the dark.

*　　*　　*

The next morning Nate searched the area again and found no sign of Chuck Shingle. There was no fresh snow, and he found only old tracks, including the girl's. He did find fresh tracks near the barn and a note in the wire box they had been leaving food for the girl in. It was written on the back of Nate's last note asking her to join them, explaining how the three together had a better chance of surviving than they would separately. Nate brought it in and gave it to Brian.

Brian's eyes lit up. "Good! It's about damn time she trusted us."

Nate regarded the excitement on Brian's face. "Now remember, I told you she's ugly, so don't be cruel when we first meet her. There's a place in this world for ugly girls too you know."

"Oh, shut up. I don't care what she looks like. She saved my life, yours too."

"I fully understand: You just want to thank her. That's why you fought me for the binocs that time when I saw her taking the rifle off that dead man."

"Probably you two will wind up married in a year, so why don't you shut up?"

Nate forced himself not to smile. "Don't you remember me telling you she's too young for me? Besides, she's ugly. Of course ugly girls get married too, just not to me. I was married to your mother, a babe, and she spoiled me, so no ugly girls for me."

Brian was not amused. "You think all of that is cute, don't you?" He looked away. "I miss Mom."

"So do I."

Brian blanched and jerked his head to look at Nate. "I didn't mean…I know you loved her."

"Well, just remember your manners and don't let on how ugly she is. After all, she saved your life." Nate turned away so Brian could not see the smile in his eyes.

*   *   *

"Maybe she was killed by Chuckey." Brian looked through bullet holes in a living room window's shutters. "She should have been here by now. It'll be dark soon."

"I haven't heard any gunfire," Nate said, "and I doubt Chuckey or anyone else is likely to sneak up on her in the woods and get her with a knife."

"Well, she's not here."

"Could be anything. Maybe she's had second thoughts about coming in and meeting us. For now I need you to help finish the laundry." Nate tossed a wet shirt to him. "It'll be good exercise since you've been laid up and have to get your muscles working again. You will need to be able to walk down to the river after I've packed everything to Mel's. I don't want to have to carry you too. Just take it easy and be careful with your leg."

Brian hung the shirt on a line Nate stretched across the back of the living room so they would not have to expose themselves to danger outside. "My leg doesn't have much strength, but it doesn't hurt."

"You'll have to rebuild your strength and stamina as far as the rest of your body is concerned. It shouldn't take long though because you've been forced to get out of bed and help me so much. You can thank Chuckey and his gang for that." He wrung out another shirt in the kitchen sink after rinsing. "Your leg is another matter. That muscle is going to bother you for some time, long after the bullet wound has healed. Getting shot is not like in the movies where people recover completely."

"But I can walk okay."

"Yes, you can walk."

Brian limped to the same window and looked through the same bullet hole and saw no sign of the girl. "It seems strange her leaving a note and then not showing up. Something is wrong."

Chapter 12

Morning broke unnaturally cold but much warmer than it had been in weeks. At least it was above freezing. Nate took a rope and led their cow into the pasture. The grass was dry, but for the morning dew, and brown from multiple freezes. The cow munched on it contentedly nonetheless. She seemed happy to be out of the stall. Afterwards, he carried feed to a trough for her.

Brian kept watch through the bedroom window, Nate's bolt-action ready for quick use. Glassing both sides of the field and pasture with binoculars, he was watching for the girl as much as Chuck Shingle. This time he was sitting in a chair and not the bed, and the steel plate was turned back on its side so it would not be too high for Brian to shoot over.

Bright, warm sunlight shined into the open barn door while Nate worked. He finished there and walked into the house. Speaking down the hall from the living room, he said, "I'm going to take a pack load down to the river. The sun is still in the east, so I will go down the east tree line back in the shadows where it's harder for anyone to see me."

"I'll watch the western side close," Brian said. "Keep a lookout for the girl."

Nate hooked a shoulder strap with an arm and swung the pack around so he could slip his left arm under a strap and pulled the pack tight against his shoulder. "Worried about her, are you?"

Brian rolled his eyes. "You know she could be in trouble, so stop being an ass."

Nate smiled. "That's no way to talk to your father. And are you rolling your eyes again? How disrespectful."

"I will apologize if you do, for picking on me."

"A father should never apologize. After all, I'm bigger than you."

"Funny."

"Don't make me go in there," Nate joked. "You need to put the bar in place after I close the door anyway."

Brian limped in. Nate was glad he remembered to take the shotgun with him. "If I see her, will tell her you're worried about her."

"Whatever," Brian said. "Be careful."

Nate walked out the door and headed across the front of the house and into the trees, rifle in hand. On his second trip down to the swamp, his eyes caught movement in the brush. He froze.

A voice came from out of the woods. "Don't shoot."

Nate recognized the girl's voice. "Watch where you point any weapons and show yourself."

She came closer, walking slowly into a six foot wide clearing. She stood there and said nothing.

"Well," Nate said. He judged her to be about twenty, perhaps a year older. *So much for judging a girl's age by her voice in the dark.* "It's about time we met. My son has been worried about you. The note said you would come in yesterday."

She took a step closer. "I came across the last one of those men you've had so much trouble with."

Nate was all ears. "You know where he is?"

"The last I saw of him he was in a boat heading downriver. Since he seemed to be leaving the area, I turned back."

Nate considered this information, thinking Shingle was heading for town to look for victims or more thugs to build a new gang with. "It's almost lunch time for us, you're invited. Why don't you come with me down to the river? I've got to pack this stuff to a cache." His eyes locked with hers. "But you already know I've been packing stuff down there, don't you? I've felt your eyes on me many times."

She nodded. "My guess is you're moving to a safer place."

"Yes. This farm is too accessible, with the road and river so close. We've been getting too many uncouth visitors lately." His face softened. "Except you: You're welcome."

Her eyes lit up slightly, but she was still wary. "Thanks."

Nate regarded her appearance, careful not to linger too long with his eyes. He did not want to give her the wrong idea. "I didn't expect you to be so clean, living out here in the woods for so long."

She smiled and he saw genuine warmth. "I cleaned up in the river this morning."

Nate noticed before that her raven hair was a little wet; now he took more account of it. "I bet that was cold."

"But I felt so much better after. These are my cleanest clothes."

They stood silently for a few seconds. She spoke first. "Where is your wife? All I've seen is you and the boy."

"Brian and I lost her and little Beth to the sickness."

"Oh, I'm so sorry. I thought, but I had to ask."

"No need to apologize, I don't mind you asking. You need to know what you're getting into. I understand."

They grew silent again. "My son is going to be surprised. I told him you are ugly."

Her reaction was so slight, he just caught it.

"I'm just pulling his leg. He turned thirteen last week." His face suddenly changed. "Damn it. I completely forgot."

"I can bake a cake," she said, "if you have the flour, sugar, milk, eggs…"

"We both would be grateful. I'm not much for baking."

She smiled, her eyes lighting up. "I even have a gift: A .22 pistol. I need the .22 rifle for small game though."

They both laughed.

"What branch?" Nate asked, his eyes appraising her reaction.

"Huh? Oh, 11 Bravo."

"Infantry rifleman."

She appraised Nate in turn. "You?"

"Infantry, Airborne Ranger. That was a lifetime ago. You didn't learn your woodsman skills in Basic."

"I guess you can blame my father for that. He turned me into a tomboy I'm afraid. Of course it was my fault too."

"Praise would be a more appropriate word. He must have been Green Beret or Delta." Nate headed downslope. "Come on; let's get this pack load in place. There's a boy who is impatient to meet the ugly girl who saved his life the other day."

"He was doing pretty well on his own."

*   *   *

"Stay back in the trees here," Nate told the woman. "Let me warn Brian we have company. I will call you when it's time."

"I guess it's safer that way. I mean, he's watching from that window with a rifle."

Nate said nothing. He just gave her a look that showed respect. "I told Brian you might be military."

*   *   *

Brian stood in the living room, gaping at her.

"Close your mouth, Son. Or are you catching flies?"

"You're a liar, Dad."

Nate glanced at her and laughed. "Gotcha, didn't I?"

"So you don't think I'm ugly?" She asked.

Brian's face turned a shade of red. "He told you what he said? No, I don't."

Nate saved him. "This is my son, Brian, and I'm Nate Williams. I'm afraid I simply forgot to ask your name out there."

She smiled warmly. "Deni Heath."

Nate showed surprise. "You're no kin to Colonel Jim Heath, are you?"

"Yes…my father."

"He's a great man. I served under him in South America, a first-class officer and decent man. We jumped from country to country, hunting terrorists." Nate shook memories from his head. "What brought you here?"

She held her chin up. "Thank you. He *was* a great man. He died early in the plague."

"I'm sorry to hear that. What a loss. We need people like him to rebuild our society."

"As to what brought me here, I was trying to get to my fiancé, but things got so chaotic I was forced to take evasive action. Travel by road is just too dangerous, so I used backcountry trails and tried to stay out of everyone's path. I am...was...on leave, I'm AWOL now, and was unarmed until I took those guns off the men you killed after they shot your son. You don't want to be unarmed out there, but you know that."

"Were you traveling by bus?" Nate asked.

"Rental car. I had to bail out during an ambush. They had the road blocked with crashed cars. I wasn't born yesterday and knew what was up, but I had to get through. So I tried to race around the jam. Lost all my baggage but what was in a small pack I grabbed when I rolled out of the car while it was still moving. A couple rednecks were shooting it to hell at the time. I hit the woods and never looked back. That was a lifetime ago. I've lost track of time. I've been in escape and evasion mode since."

"That crazy crap finally came in handy, huh?"

"Yeah."

"And you stuck around because of our handouts?"

She seemed to be thinking about that. "Partly. I felt safer here. I mean, you two are the only people I've seen in weeks who did not act like they were insane. You helped me, and then when trouble came to you, I felt I owed you, so I stuck around even after it wasn't so safe here anymore." She looked inward. "The fact is I probably can't make it to North Carolina. It's just too dangerous to travel right now. It's crazy, I tell you. Maybe in a few months." She gave a wintry smile. "So here I am."

"Like I said before, you're welcome. We can use another pair of hands and eyes for security. That's more important at the moment than supplies. Pulling security is a lot less tiring when it's divided among three instead of two."

"I can do more than that, like help on the farm." Her eyes flashed to Brian and back to Nate. "And bake."

"Bake?" Brian broke in. "He bakes biscuits."

"Well, let me cook lunch," Nate said. "Maybe you can cook tonight, if you're not too tired. I would like for you to help me pack stuff to the river after lunch. Brian is back on his feet, but his leg hasn't healed completely yet. It was bad for a while: infection."

"Oh boy," Deni said. "That's dangerous with no hospitals." She eyed his bandaged leg. "I have some medical training, just a little, wasn't my MOS, but I might could help."

"No need, it's okay now," Brian offered a little too eagerly. "Really, Dad has taken care of it."

Nate winked at Deni. "Yeah, we Williams men don't show our legs to just any girl that shows up you know."

Brian turned red. "Oh shut up! You never quit."

"Why don't you two have a seat while I cook?" Nate headed for the kitchen.

Deni sat on a nearby couch. "Well, what *is* for lunch anyway? I hope it's not rabbit."

Brian dropped into a chair as if someone had just popped his ego balloon. "Eggs and wild hog, I'm sure. That's what we had this morning, yesterday, the day before, and the day before."

"Sounds good to me."

"It won't after a few days," they both said in unison.

She pointed, a big disarming smile on her face. "See, I can read minds."

They both laughed.

She was winning Brian over already.

*   *   *

"Is it really *that* bad out there?" Nate asked. He drank milk from a glass and forked another bite of egg into his mouth.

Deni relished the warm food, tasting every morsel. It was the first time she had eaten at a table in months. "I don't think I need to convince you how crazy it is after all you two have been through. You're out here in the country; imagine what it's like where there are more people to go crazy on you." She looked across the table at Nate. "America has become Somalia: a total breakdown of society. I'll leave it at that. I don't want to get explicit at the table."

Nate stopped eating. "I knew it would be bad with no law, but... So the damn fools are turning a tragedy into an even worse disaster." He looked at Brian with worried eyes.

"There must be enough good people out there with some sense who will help us rebuild."

"Sure. Someday," Deni's voice lacked confidence. "I mean, in a few years, sure we'll rebuild."

Nate's jaw set. He stood, leaving food on the plate. "There's work to be done, and I might as well get to it." He started to walk into the living room to fill his pack for another trip to the river but turned back to them. "Brian is going to have a life. If that means the whole country must be rebuilt from the ground up, so be it." He went to work loading his pack. "People have got to act like Americans again. What happened to the Americans who stopped the Nazis and Nipponese? The pioneers who settled wilderness with no help from any government, just a few good neighbors, or no one? This fall started long before the sickness came. The sickness is bad, but what we have done to ourselves is much worse. Hell, maybe we caused the sickness."

Deni swallowed, glanced at Brian, and got up. She leaned over and whispered in Brian's ear. "Your father loves you, never doubt it."

Brian blinked. "It took you long enough to figure that out."

She touched Brian's face lightly and kissed him on his cheek, turning his face red. "I'm slow, you have to excuse me." She smiled and headed for the living room. "Got an extra pack? Mine's too small to carry much."

Nate motioned with his head while stuffing canned goods into his pack. "Brian's, it's already loaded."

*   *   *

They managed six trips before Nate decided to rest. He was worried about her being tired. But he had to admit he was all done in himself, having gone with little or no sleep for so long, and someone had to stand watch so Brian could sleep.

The cow was locked in its stall for the night.

Deni wanted the first watch, but Nate argued he should pull security first while she rested. "It will be nice to sleep the darkest hours for a change," he said. "You can take from two to daylight."

Nate looked out the bedroom window, glassing the tree line on both sides of the field and pasture, when he heard clanging in the kitchen. He had an idea what she was doing. A delicious aroma confirmed it thirty minutes later. He wondered how successful she would be. After all, how many women are used to baking with a wood burning stove? They had been using wood to conserve what gas they had.

Deni walked in. She spoke with a low voice so Brian would not be awakened. "I used nearly all of the last of your sugar, but it's finished. Couldn't find any small candles for the cake though."

"I don't think we have any small candles. We have a few larger ones left, but no small ones. Thanks for that. You must be dead on your feet, and you take the time to bake a cake for a kid you just met today."

She smiled. "Oh, we met a long time ago. In a way, we three have been in combat together. We're old chums."

Something came to Nate. "Why did it take you so long to trust us enough to come in? It just seems that once you finally decided to join us, you have left behind all doubts about us."

"That's because I was convinced of what kind of person you are *before* I walked out of the woods. I have learned lately to be very careful about dealing with people. I'm sure about you and have no reservations about being your friend." She looked away melodramatically and wiped a faux tear from her eye. "Besides, I think I'm in love with your son."

Nate laughed. "Well, watch it. He may fall in love with you. He's just old enough to fall for an older woman. He doesn't need his heart broken. There is more than enough for him to deal with now without those kinds of growing pains."

She pretended to be hurt. "An older woman? Just how old do you think I am?"

"About twenty or so." Nate's eyes narrowed. "So you're about young enough to be my daughter if I had married young."

She changed her stance and tilted her head. Her eyes bored into him. "I'm twenty-four. You can check my driver's license if you want proof." She held up her hand, displaying an engagement diamond. "I'm very much devoted to my fiancé. Being the friendly type, guys often get the wrong idea. You can imagine the trouble that caused in the Army."

"Yes, I can. Around here you will be treated like a good friend...one of the guys, so to speak. No need to worry about me getting the wrong idea. I'm still in love with Susan and a hurting widower. I'm just asking that you keep in mind Brian's vulnerabilities. Present circumstances and your beauty add to the problem."

"Do you want me to be cold to him? That may be worse than him developing a crush."

"No, be yourself, just keep a look out for any sign he is starting to think of you as a girlfriend rather than an adult friend. Bring up how devoted you are to your fiancé and talk as if you're already married. Make it clear to him you're already happy with your future husband. Maybe that will stop him from getting carried away with juvenile fantasies."

"That seems like a good idea."

"You better get some sleep. It will be your watch in a few hours."

"Okay, but don't touch that cake. Brian gets the first piece."

They both smiled.

Chapter 13

The morning sun inched up in the east and strained to penetrate misting fog. Deni yawned and put the binoculars to her eyes, glassing the tree line on the western side. She saw no movement.

Nate forced his eyes open and swung his booted feet onto the hardwood floor. It was difficult to tell with all the windows shuttered, but it seemed like daylight outside. The birds sang, but they often start their chorus before sunrise, like roosters. He sat up on the living room couch, holstered his revolver, which he held in his right hand the whole time he slept, and shook sleep from his head. Before he got out of the couch, he grabbed his M14 and checked the chamber and magazine to be certain both were full.

Nate heard movement in the kitchen and wondered why Deni left her post. He looked in and found Brian sitting at the table, drinking coffee. Brian got up and poured Nate a cup from the pot on the woodstove, limping along the way.

Nate started to tell him to stay seated, but then thought that Brian needed to move around and start getting some exercise. He sat across the table. "You didn't need to get up so early, Deni's on watch. You will be in there glassing all day while we pack more stuff to the river."

"I can handle that okay. All I'll be doing is sitting there looking out the window."

"*If* no one shows up. Like Chuckey. And remember, you can't just shoot anyone you see. The men we have had trouble with are dead. Chuckey is the only one left. Keep your eyes open and your head working. If they are a threat to us do not hesitate to kill them, but don't shoot until you know."

"I know that, Dad." Brian had something on his mind. "Do you still think it's necessary to move to the bunker? That thing is going to be hotter than hell this summer. And we really need to put in a crop."

"Yes, it's still necessary. There will be more people coming out here from town and even other parts of the country. Many will not be thugs, but they will be hungry, and hungry, frightened people do nasty things. At the very least, we will be overwhelmed with people asking for a handout. If we say no, we had better be capable of handling them when they decide to stop asking…and some of them will. I would like to help, but we just do not have the supplies to feed thousands." His face hardened. "We must move to the bunker, Brian. We have no choice."

"If someone finds us there, we will be stuck in that thing."

"I would rather be stuck there than in this house." Nate put his cup down. "We have survived a kind of siege here, so we can certainly handle one there."

Brian looked into his black coffee. "I hate leaving our farm."

"So do I, it's why I waited so long to make up my mind to move."

"It was me getting shot that did it."

"It was reality, the way things are." Nate sat back in his chair, his coffee forgotten. "More people are coming, many of them dangerous. You heard what she said last night. It is total anarchy."

Brian lost interest his coffee also. "We can grow food here and keep the chickens and cow. We can't do that at Mel's."

"When we come back, there may be nothing left but the land." Nate saw the reaction on Brian's face. "But we can rebuild. The land is what will feed us in the future. We have seeds stored and so does Mel."

"We are going to leave Mom and Beth."

Nate swallowed. "Brian, they left us when they died. They're gone. No one is going to bother the graves. They might burn the markers for heat, but we can replace that too."

"Are we taking the tools with us?"

"Yes, we will need them when we start farming again." Nate tried to read his son's face.

"The truck and tractor will be gone or destroyed. How are we going to till the land?"

"That's why we are taking everything we can. That old plow that Grandpa used when he was young will work with me pulling and you walking behind."

Brian was astonished. "You can't carry that thing down to the river and then uphill to Mel's bunker, it's too heavy!"

"I will bury it back in the trees. I can carry it that far."

"You can't pull it either." Brian became more insistent. "You need a mule to pull it."

Nate smiled and shook his head. "You're just full of worry and argument this morning, aren't you?"

Brian was not finished. "And the handles will rot if you bury it."

"Okay, let's see...I'm going to remove the handles and take them with us. During the Depression, women pulled plows while their husbands walked behind, so I think I can do it. We may be able to trade for a mule sometime in the future." Nate sat back in his chair and crossed his arms. "Anything else bothering you?"

"You don't want to hear it anyway." Brian suddenly had a renewed interest in his coffee.

"I asked because I *do* want to know what's on your mind."

Brian looked up at his father and then into his coffee again. "I want to stay here."

Nate could not believe it. "I just went through the reasons we can't stay. Brian, there's just no way."

Brian exploded out of his chair and rushed into his room as fast as his leg would let him.

Nate sat there confused. *What is wrong with him, really?* He looked around the table and saw, in his mind's eye, Susan and Beth sitting there laughing and happy. *This home is the place we were a whole family, the last place he was happy. It's the last connection to Susan and Beth.* Nate rubbed his forehead hard and ran his shaking hand down his unshaven face. He shook with rage at the world for hurting his son and killing his wife and daughter. Then he slammed his fist down on the table. The coffee cup vibrated, spilling some of its contents. *We have no choice!*

Deni ran in. "I...heard something." She saw it in his eyes.

Nate looked up to see Brian hobble into the kitchen and stop behind her, shotgun in hand. His face was streaked. Nate stood and forced a smile. "Sorry if I alarmed you two. Deni, will you show Brian the gift you made for him? We will be busy backpacking later, so now is as good a time as any."

Deni looked surprised, but recovered. "Sure." She put the rifle against a nearby wall. "I hid it so he couldn't stumble on it last night." She gave Brian an impish look, "It would have spoiled the surprise."

Brian stared at the chocolate cake she placed on the table. It was smaller than the cakes his mother baked, because of the scarcity of ingredients, but it reminded him of her anyway.

Deni bowed and motioned towards the table. "A little late, but it's your birthday cake. It's all yours. I'll beat your father off it if he tries to pilfer a piece."

Astonished, Brian stood there holding the shotgun. "Of all the things to do at a time like this." He looked up at her. "You don't even know me. And you lose sleep when you're so tired just to bake a cake for me?"

"Oh, it wasn't that much of a sacrifice. It was your father's idea." She crossed the room. "Let me take that." She took the shotgun and set it by the rifle. Leading him to the table, she said, "I will fix breakfast. You can have some cake and milk for desert."

Brian sat down. "I can't eat all of it. Both of you might as well have some."

"I'm going to rig the steel plate in that window," Nate said. "We will eat and enjoy some of the cake before Deni and I start work."

Deni said, "It won't go bad you know. You can eat a piece after every meal for a couple days. I did bake it for you. It will probably be your last cake for a long while."

"Thanks." Brian gave her a shy smile.

"You're welcome." She snapped her fingers. "I'll be back." She scurried off down the hall, leaving Brian sitting at the table.

Deni came back holding a .22 pistol. "Your father cleaned it last night." She handed it to Brian. "It's all I can give you."

Brian examined it. "Wow. It's a Ruger with target sights and a bull barrel." He looked up. "The one you took off that guy?"

Deni shrugged. "It's all I have to give."

Brian seemed pleased and perplexed at the same time. "I never expected Dad to make a big deal out of my birthday with everything he's had to deal with. *I* even forgot that I turned thirteen, we've been so busy. And you, a stranger, go and act like you've known me for years. You must be a really great person."

Her eyes shined. "You bet I'm a great person. But your father did not forget. Who do you think told me about your birthday?"

Nate put a brick of .22s on the table. "Like her, I'm kind of limited as far as what I can give you."

Brian grew serious. "What you gave Mom and Beth and me has always been unlimited. No one ever had a better dad."

Deni said, "You're going to make your dad cry."

*   *   *

Nate carried the outboard, threading it between close-growing trees.

Deni had a gallon can of fuel in one hand, a rifle in the other. They both carried heavy packs on their backs. "Are you still going to take a load upriver? It looks like rain."

"No," Nate said. "A cold front is coming in. It will storm before dark. I'll wait until tomorrow."

"I think we can make one more trip before it rains." Deni looked at the sky.

"Yep. Rain's not going to stop me though. You can stay in the house while I keep hauling stuff down here."

"You forget I'm Army. Don't baby me."

Nate shrugged. "Your choice."

"Okay. Where is this place you're moving to? I mean, besides upriver."

"It belongs to a friend of ours. He was called in when the plague started. We haven't heard from him since."

"Called in?" Deni asked.

"ANG."

"Oh. Well, chances are he didn't make it. Sorry to tell you, but it's true."

"No way to know, but you're probably right." Nate walked around a large palmetto frond.

They managed to complete two more trips. Nate looked out the window as he stood by Brian who was sitting in the chair, glassing the scene with binoculars. "We will get wet on the next haul."

Deni asked, "Where's that poncho?" The sky in the northwest was woolly with heavy clouds and growing darker by the minute. A few drops blew in through the window. "Here it comes."

Brian lowered the binoculars. "It's going to rain in and there's no glass to stop it."

Nate turned the steel plate on its end, covering all but the upper few inches of the opening.

"It's still going to rain in and run down the plate, Dad."

"It doesn't matter," Nate said. "And you won't be able to see anything out there anyway, so you might as well go eat some more cake or read."

"It will ruin the floor."

Nate said nothing. He looked away.

Brian's eyes flashed to Deni. "He talks like the two go together or something: If you read you *got* to eat cake, if you eat cake you *got* to read."

Deni forced a laugh. "Yeah."

"Let's eat supper and get back to work." Nate disappeared down the hall.

After supper, Nate and Deni loaded packs and headed down to the river.

"I thought it couldn't possibly rain any harder a few minutes ago," Deni said. "Now I'm wondering if this isn't a new record for rainfall per hour."

A lightning bolt struck a tall dead pine on the other side of the field and wind drove sheets of cold rain in their face.

Nate tried to see more than ten feet ahead and was having little luck. "It will save us time, so it's worth it."

"How is that?"

"No one will see us in this heavy rain and dark. We can walk in the open and not have to deal with the trees and brush."

"Are you planning on working all night to take advantage of the cover of this weather?"

"Yes, but you should stay with Brian tonight, get some rest."

She walked faster. "No. I can outwork any Ranger."

"Suit yourself."

On the next trip it was storming so strong and the night so dark, Nate and Deni felt it safe to use the tractor without being seen. They loaded two one hundred pound propane tanks and several twenty pound tanks onto the trailer. They also took the kerosene refrigerator and other heavy items, such as a generator and even the woodstove. Brian helped load as best he could, limping around the house, donning a poncho and joining them in the cold rain until Nate ordered him inside. "You're not well yet and a candidate for pneumonia," he said.

By morning they had everything Nate planned to bring to Mel's retreat hidden in the swamp not far from the river. He still had not decided what to do with the cow and whether or not they could keep the chickens at Mel's and still not be found. The animals could not be kept in the bunker with them or in the cave, and the chickens would be noisy and attract attention. The cow would have to be released to fend for itself or butchered for meat. He knew Brian did not like either idea. The most humane thing to do was kill it. Without someone to relieve her udder, she would be in pain in only a few days.

By two AM, it stormed with increasing violence outside while Brian slept. Nate opened Susan's dresser. He turned to Deni. "Take anything practicable that you can use. Susan was taller and a little larger than you, but I think you can wear her stuff. There are jeans and shirts. Take cold weather stuff too for next winter. Spring is breaking now, or it should be, but you will need them next winter. There are a couple pair of good work boots. None of her stuff is going to fit you for town, but you're not going to be socializing anytime soon and we won't be appraising your clothing."

Deni gave him a look only a woman can. "Thank you for being so kind."

"You're welcome. But anything we leave behind will most likely be lost anyway."

"That's not what I meant. This is your wife's things."

He looked away. "Put what you want to take with us in plastic garbage bags so they won't get wet. Hurry, we need to take advantage of the cover of this storm while we can." He left the room, closing the door behind him in case she wanted to check Susan's clothes for fit.

Deni picked anything in green she could find that would be good work clothes. She discarded anything bright colored that would make her easy to see in the woods. Blue jeans were acceptable for their practicality, but she would rather they were olive drab or even camouflage patterned. She was happy to find a half dozen dull green T-shirts that were just baggy enough for active wear.

Brian got out of bed and followed Nate into the kitchen.

"You need to be sleeping," Nate told Brian.

Brian rubbed his eyes until they adjusted to the lamplight. "I can't."

"Well, if you're not going to sleep, put all your clothes in garbage bags and pile them near the front door. Make sure you take all your boots and socks. This will be about the last night we spend here."

Brian collapsed into a chair in the living room and stared at the closed front door. He said nothing, but Nate knew what he was thinking.

"Best to move fast now," Nate said. "We're in an awkward position with all our stuff down by the river and us still in the house. That storm is not going to last much longer."

Brian pushed himself up out of the chair as if he were made of lead.

Nate grabbed a few garbage bags and followed him to his room. "Let's get your stuff bagged and on the flatbed trailer."

Brian went about the chore in a funk, without a word. Nate was happy to see him working with speed, and they soon had his room cleaned out of anything useful to Brian's survival. Brian picked his birthday present off a dresser and started to stuff it under his belt. He had no holster for it.

"Wait. Is it loaded?" Nate asked. "The chamber, I mean."

"Yes."

Nate took it from him, removed the magazine, ejected the chambered round onto the bed, put it in the magazine, and then pushed the magazine in and handed it back to Brian. "That pistol is a squirrel gun, or a last-ditch weapon. Don't rely on the safety when you're carrying a pistol like that. I carried a .45 cocked and locked most of the time I was in a combat zone, but not with it pointed at my privates, stuck in my paints. You need a holster. Keep the mag. loaded and the chamber empty."

"Okay."

Nate checked the nearly empty dresser and closet to make certain they were not leaving something behind Brian would need. Then he looked under the bed. There, he found an old pair of athletic shoes. "Put that in the bag with your extra boots."

They started down the hall, each with a full bag. "Careful not to put a hole in it," Nate warned.

Deni was outside, carrying a bag to the trailer, so Nate went out the door with his bag. Brian started to follow. "No. Stay at the door, off to the side so no one can see you, and I will take it the rest of the way. No need for you to get wet."

Brian stayed in the house while the other two used the tractor to haul their last load of the night down to the river and hide it in the woods.

As soon as they got back, Nate unhooked the trailer and attached the cultivator. He plowed under a few acres and raised the discs before driving the tractor around the field to make it appear it was used for farm work and not to haul trailer loads to the river. The field was soft and muddy. He was afraid the tractor's tracks would be noticeable come daylight.

There was still work to do. Nate and Deni prepared food to last a day so they could work from sunup to sundown without wasting time to cook, and then went to bed. They fell asleep within seconds.

Brian stood watch, just sitting in the living room listening to the wind and rain. He yawned and got up to walk around, trying to stay awake. His mood was as gloomy as the night.

He sat back in the couch and was starting to lose his battle with fatigue when a sound outside sent him exploding to his feet. Brian was certain he heard the tractor start up.

Chapter 14

The front wall of the living room caved in. Cold wind blasted Brian's face, and rain drenched the floor. A bolt of lightning lit up the yard outside for a second, silhouetting a hulking form that protruded into the house. Brian fired as soon as his shotgun touched his shoulder. A human form jumped off the tractor just as he pulled the trigger. Brian continued to fire through the hole, hoping to hit the man, until his shotgun was empty.

Nate ran in, his rifle shouldered.

Brian was reloading. He answered before Nate could ask. "I'm all right. It must be Chuckey."

Deni raced down the hall, rifle at the low ready, stopping just inside the living room.

Nate appraised the scene. "Someone hot-wired the tractor and drove it through the wall." He shouted at Deni more than Brian, who grabbed shells from a box on the end table and stuffed them in his pockets.

Nate was furious with himself. "Son of a bitch! I forgot to disable the tractor when I parked it. I took the keys, but—"

"The house doesn't matter anymore, Dad."

"That's not the point."

"People make mistakes when they're as tired as you," Deni said.

"There is no excuse. You two go to bed. I will stand watch the rest of the night."

"No." Brian yelled above the raging storm. "You two are the ones who need rest. I can handle it."

"Brian, he's out there."

"I'll be okay because he can only shoot through the hole and the tractor covers most of it."

The wind shifted and more rain blew in, soaking much of the furniture on that side of the room.

Nate walked to his poncho that was hanging by the front door and slipped it on.

"Dad, don't!"

Nate pointed. "Get over there and be quiet and stay inside no matter what."

"I won't. If you go, I won't stay. Just rest, I can keep him out till morning."

Nate rushed across the room and shook Brian by his shoulders. "Do what I tell you!"

"No. He wants you outside. He's waiting."

"He may think he wants me out there, but he doesn't."

"Don't go," Brian said. "Please, not tonight. He has something planned. I know it."

"Of course he does. He might know where we left our supplies. If he's been around all night, that's more than likely."

"Let me go guard the supplies until morning," Deni said.

"No." Nate crawled under the tractor and searched the dark, wet night. After waiting several minutes for lightning to light the yard and seeing nothing but streaming sheets of hard rain, he crawled back into the room. "Stay alert. I'll be back in a minute." He returned with his load-bearing harness and pistol belt over his poncho and his backpack which he carried by the shoulder straps. He went into the kitchen, filled a two-quart canteen from a pail of water, took what food was left in the house, and returned to the living room. "Load up anything you have left in the house you do not want to leave behind. We are abandoning the house right now. There is nothing here worth dying for."

Brian nearly yelled, "The chickens and cow!"

"Like I said, there is nothing left here worth dying for."

Brian was not giving up. "I know you're as tired of eggs as me, but fresh eggs are a lot better than Mel's freeze-dried stuff any day."

"There is no time to argue," Nate said. "You two need to be ready to leave in a few minutes."

Deni rushed into the bedroom she was sleeping in.

Brian kicked a chair across the room and then started getting ready to leave. "I came *so* close to killing the bastard."

"Fill your canteen," Nate said. He looked through the hole into the storm.

Deni walked into the kitchen, already in a poncho and with her pack on, the .22 rifle tied to it, her fighting rifle in her hands. She filled her canteens and then took Brian's and filled them.

Nate waited until they returned to the living room. Just able to see them in the dark, he came closer and whispered, "Come with me." They walked down the hall into Brian's bedroom. Nate turned and whispered, "We're going out through the window. I'm going first. I will go into the woods and make sure it's clear. If you don't hear any shots after five minutes, Brian goes next. Brian, you wait by the window against the wall. Stay low until Deni gets out. Then both of you run straight into the woods. I'll be waiting and keeping watch. After that, we will go deeper into the woods and swing around to the cache and load the water tank for the first trip."

First, Nate removed the window screen. When he opened the shutter, the roar of wind and hammering of rain on the tin roof was loud in the room. It was not letting up, if anything the storm grew stronger. The window was not large enough, so he took his pack off and had Deni push it through after he was outside.

A lightning bolt lit his surroundings, trees danced in the wind, creating a macabre scene. Nate rushed to the trees and searched the area as best he could in the wet, storm-tossed miasma. Someone could have been out there in the woods and Nate not see him, but the same storm also kept Nate hidden.

Five minutes later, Brian was waiting against the wall. Then Deni pushed her pack out and Brian pulled it out of the way. She slipped through the window onto the ground. They ran into the brush and stopped because they could see nothing.

Nate spoke just loud enough they could hear three feet away. "Brian, grab my pack. Deni, grab his. You two follow along behind me. I will go slow." *As if there were any other way in this mess.* He worried about the danger of a windblown tree falling on them. Nate saw two trees down in the yard when lightning lifted the curtain of darkness earlier. *It may be a slow moving cold front, but it looks like a hurricane.*

With compass in one hand, its needle and cardinal points glowing in the dark, rifle in the other, Nate took them deeper into the woods and then swung around to head downslope. He held his rifle out to protect his eyes from branches and felt his way with the toes of his boots.

Nate purposely kept to the left enough they would reach the river downstream, so he would know what direction to turn when they got there. They made their way upriver until he came to a small creek that had been dry before the storm but now was swollen and overflowing.

"Wait here," Nate said. "I'm going to scout the area before we get any closer."

He returned thirty minutes later. "It's clear." They walked upslope until they came to their cache.

Nate turned to them. "Take your packs off and wait. You will hear me coming because I'll be pulling that water tank through the brush."

"Let me help you," Brian said.

"No. You two wait here." Nate took his pack off and set it on the tarpaulin covering all their worldly possessions, then left them in the dark.

Fifteen minutes later, Nate pulled the tank past them and slid it into the water. He loaded a half dozen ammunition cans and plastic bags of canned goods in the bottom of the tank and attached the outboard to one end.

Nate stood in the creek as they handed him more items to load.

Brian handed him a gallon fuel can. "Can't we load more than that? It will be easier than packing it."

"No. It will sink too deep and mire in the muddy bottom."

Deni and Brian carried as much as they could manage while Nate pulled the tank to the river by rope from the bank, floating it down the engorged creek. Brian hobbled, trying to keep as much strain off his leg as possible.

"Unload your packs into the tank and we'll get another load." Nate arranged the heaviest items so they would be on the bottom and keep the tank's center of gravity low. As soon as they were done, all three headed for the cache. "Be as quiet as possible and stay alert." Nate's voice was just audible above the roar of the storm.

When they got to the cache, Deni said, "Just in case you need it later, that canoe is on this side of the river where it bends sharply to the south. There's a spring flowing into the river there. It's where I've been getting my drinking water."

Brian broke in. "He doesn't need the canoe, he's coming with us."

Nate ignored Brian. "Thanks, I will need it tomorrow if everything works out tonight."

"Good luck," Deni said.

Five more trips and the tank was setting lower in the water as it strained against its bowline and danced in the swift current. Deni used her hands in the dark to determine how much of the tank was still above water. "I think it will take more. Certainly there is more room for lighter stuff."

"No," Nate said. "You two are taking it upriver. Brian, go to the creek below Mel's place and walk to the bunker. Leave everything but your weapons and packs in the tank. Just tie it off well and pull it up on the bank as far as you can in case it fills with rainwater." He handed Brian the keys. "You know how to get past his security."

"No!" Brian said. "You're coming with us."

"I have a little more experience at this, Brian. And there is no time to argue." Nate handed Deni a spotlight he took out of the water tank. "You ride in front. Brian will handle the kicker. Brian, you will have to tell her when you're close to that creek so she can turn the light on to search for it. Don't use the light until you're close."

"This is bullshit." Brian's voice was loud and angry. "We should stay together."

"Lower your voice," Nate said. "No, just shut up. There is no time to coddle you. Get in the tank."

Deni put her arm over Brian's shoulder. "He knows what he's doing. We have to go. He is safer in this dark without us."

"Bullshit!"

She pulled Brian towards the water tank. "He doesn't have to worry about shooting one of us in the dark if we are not here. Believe me, he is safer without us."

"I'm not going." Brian would not move. He jerked away from her.

Nate slung his rifle across his back, waded into the water, and held the tank closer to shore. "Deni, get in the front."

When she was sitting on a pile of ammunition cans, Nate walked to Brian. "Get in."

"No!"

Nate yanked the shotgun out of Brian's hands and put it in the water tank next to the outboard. Brian started to fight him, but he pinned his arms behind his back, then stunned him with a vicious slap and jerked him bodily to the edge of the river, lifted and dropped him in. Shaking Brian violently, he said, "Crank that kicker and get out of here. You have to stop being so self-centered. What about her? She doesn't know how to get to Mel's or open the bunker. Now act like a man and help her."

Brian was too stunned to say anything. Nate had never hit him before.

Nate said, "Don't stand up. Stay low to keep the tank from turning over. Now go. Stay in the bunker and wait for me."

Brian pulled the rope several times, but the motor did not start. The gas was old and the engine reluctant.

Nate waded back in the water and turned the outboard so he could adjust the choke and pull the starter rope. On the second try, he had the motor running. He eased the choke open and the motor idled smoothly after a few minutes. He shoved the water tank into deeper water. Brian put the outboard in gear and twisted its throttle.

Nate stood knee-deep and watched them be swallowed by the dark. He hated Chuck Shingle more than ever.

First, Nate took his poncho off and stuffed it in his pack and jumped up and down to make certain nothing in his load made noise. It took some time for him to get used to the cold rain. Once his clothes were soaked, he stopped shivering in the wind.

By the time Nate sat on a log and peered into the dark and rain towards the house, he knew the storm was waning. Rain came down in sheets, but the wind had slacked off and the brooding gloom of the woods was still but for the torrent that now fell straight down. Soon it would be perfect for hunting.

The crack of a rifle shot caused Nate to flinch and involuntarily slide off the log onto his stomach. He was ready when another rifle shot sliced the night and saw the muzzle flash back in trees across the field. *He doesn't know we're not in the house. I got you, you son of a bitch! Keep shooting.*

Slowly, he crawled into the open and headed for the other side of the field. Another shot cracked, and glass shattered from a window. He prayed the rain would continue until he reached the tree line on Shingle's side.

When he was across the field and in cover, Nate stood and started the hunt. Flowing through brush and seeking out darkest shade, he silently walked on soggy leaves. Thunder rolled from miles away. The rain tapered off to a drizzle. Then it stopped, leaving the woods dripping and nearly windless.

There was no more shooting. Shingle was no longer where he was when he last shot. Now the odds were not so much in Nate's favor. *Come on; take another potshot at the house, asshole.* He held his rifle tighter and moved on, searching, all senses on high intensity. All of his will focused on surviving, he did not want to leave Brian alone in this broken world where all the Chuck Shingles had free rein. He never wanted to be a cop. *But tonight I am the law.*

Water dripped from trees above and crashed onto palmetto fronds, sounding like rifle shots to Nate's tension-heightened ears. Slowly, but steadily, his hunting ground grayed to increasing light in the sunless morning. The sky broke clear ahead of the coming sunrise, and it grew much colder.

He had no idea where Shingle was.

Nate took an hour to work his way around to the back of the farm. From the trees, he could see the open bedroom window they used to sneak out of the house hours ago. Once more, he searched the wall of dripping green surrounding him. There was something about a two-foot area off to his left that caught his attention. Leaves carpeted the ground; fresh, moist dirt had been kicked up along with leaves. He searched further until he came across a spot of bare earth.

Boot tracks.

Shingle saw the open window. He knows we are not in the house.

Nate moved on.

Now the hunt really begins.

Nate checked for tracks only every fifty feet, keeping most of his attention on the wall of green where death could be hiding, waiting. He knew where Shingle was going. He also knew Shingle could circle back and wait in ambush. Shingle was not smart, but he was vicious, and that viciousness gave him a predator's cunning.

To be safe, Nate kept further back in the trees from the edge of his field and pasture and off to the side of Shingle's trail. He stopped and glassed the field down towards the river. Sunrise was breaking and three does were feeding near the far tree line: their backdoor retreat to the safety of cover. Fog misted above the winter-brown grass. One doe jerked her head up, looking. The other two noticed and stopped feeding, looking in the same direction. They were not looking at Nate.

Their tails lifted halfway. Standing as statues, they continued to look. One lost interest after thirty seconds, flicked its tail, and started feeding again. Then the second and third also lost interest and began to feed.

Shingle was near the cache.

Beat you to it, you son of a bitch. They're gone; it's just you and me.

Nate continued the death hunt.

Ever slower, Nate eased through the woods, searching every inch of the brooding, wet gloom before each step.

Death loomed close. It was a matter of who saw who first and who got off the first accurate shot.

Where will Chuckey wait for his chance to kill me?

Chapter 15

Shingle was not there. Nate had to admit to himself that simple fact. He circled the area from the cache to the rain-flooded swamp. Shingle had kept away from the cache and circled, getting just close enough to see that some of the supplies were gone and no one was around. Tracks led upriver.

Nate's heart rate jumped. *Does he know about Mel's place?*

Resisting an urge to run Shingle down, which would be Nate's death warrant, as he was likely to blunder into an ambush, Nate followed Shingle's trail, tension bridling his nerves. A strange, paradoxical sense of urgent energy and weariness overtook Nate. Kill Shingle and his worries would be over. But he knew that was ridiculous. There were more Shingles to come. Days of worry over Brian's fate suddenly culminated and pressed down on him. There had been no time to grieve for his loss. The living son was paramount to grief over the loss of wife and daughter. They were past pain and life on this earth. Brian still had a chance. What if he kills Shingle? More like him are surely to come in this lawless land of disease, hunger, and death. He had been a soldier in two wars, serving a year in one and then the other, but then he knew he only needed to do his duty and survive long enough and his war would come to an end. He would have the rest of his life to live in peace. That knowing had kept his resolve strong. This was a war with no end, no victory, no peace to look forward to as reward for his troubles. There was only Brian and his own belligerent will to see Brian have his chance for a life that someday may come…if the human race gets its act together and rebuilds.

Nate thought it ironic that his problem was tyranny through lack of government, but he remembered well the story of his grandfather's fight with the tyranny of government under Nazis and his near fight with tyranny here in America. A fight he called off out of love for his wife. Nate's connection with his grandfather was never closer or stronger. The fact his grandfather died in World War II, long before Nate was born mattered little.

The squelching of someone walking through mud, sinking deep and pulling his boots out, interrupted his mental storm. Nate froze. *Concentrate on staying alive, fool!* Whoever it was, Nate could not see him through the dripping wall of green. He squatted, getting low, to look under the brush.

Nothing.

Shingle was too far ahead.

Nate tried to gain on him while moving quietly through the woods. Shingle was not being so quiet and had an advantage of speed. He would never catch up with Shingle this way.

The temperature dropped and the air grew colder now that the front had passed and the skies cleared, and Nate's clothes were still wet. He shivered and continued to stalk.

When the sun was high, and the woods no longer dripping, Nate found where Shingle had turned from the river and headed upslope to higher ground. It would have been a perfect place to ambush him if only Nate had been able to get there sooner. He resisted the urge to rush ahead. Following Shingle's tracks, keeping off to the side, he paralleled the trail.

The tracks climbed out of the swamp, coming to water oaks, palmettos, and pines. Nate noticed more and more wild hog tracks as he worked his way upslope. The hogs had fled the flooded lowland for better feeding areas. A gray ghost slipped past him, its white wail raised fully as a warning flag for other deer. The buck never saw Nate, his attention was on Shingle. Ahead, he heard the grunting of feeding hogs, rooting up old acorns. Shingle was between the hogs and Nate. So close, but Nate still could not get a glimpse of Shingle because the woods were so thick.

A boar rumbled, low and throaty. Shingle cursed. "Shit. Get out of here before I shoot your ass."

When Shingle spoke, the woods came alive with panicked hogs running in all directions, squealing, grunting, and crashing through the brush. Nate rushed in for the kill, using the confusion and noise to close on Shingle. A sow nearly ran Nate over as she fled. Nate dodged and kept running. He pushed through palmettos, and came to an open area torn up by rooting hogs.

There was Shingle, standing on a windfall and pointing his rifle at a rumbling boar, its hair standing up straight, tusks clashing. The boar circled around and Shingle followed it with his rifle, turning on the log.

Nate was already aiming and starting to squeeze the trigger. Shingle's eyes caught Nate standing there and grew large with fear, his deformed face looking more grotesque than Nate remembered it. He got his rifle halfway up before Nate fired. Shingle fell, collapsed, his rifle firing into the ground. The boar fled. All before Nate's shot stopped reverberating through the surrounding trees and rolling down to the river.

For a short moment, the woods were silent. The clamor of the hogs was gone. Nate could not see Shingle where he had fallen behind the windfall. He fired at the top of the log as he approached, bullets sending wood fragments into the air, hoping to keep him down so he could not fire back. He veered to his left just before jumping over the log, firing as he came over, landing on his left side.

Shingle was not there.

Nate saw blood. *Damn!* In his haste to get off the shot, he had only wounded. He could tell by the color of the blood that it was not a lung shot; otherwise it would be pinker. He rolled several feet and then crawled on his belly to brush. Bullets slammed into a pine tree, just over his head. Nate flattened against the ground and then crawled to better cover.

Not risking exposing himself by raising his head to search for Shingle, Nate crawled farther into thick brush, not making a sound. Here he waited. *Okay asshole, you got lucky, but I'm going to kill you today.*

Nate heard crashing in the brush. Shingle ran, heading back to the swamp. Nate got to his knees and saw a flash of movement. He threw the rifle to his shoulder and aimed at an opening in the brush, not four feet wide, just ahead of

Shingle's path. Again, a flash of movement. Nate fired three quick shots.

A heavy object splashed in standing water. A moan reached Nate's ears. He smiled. The smile vanished when a shot rang out. *Damn it! Can't I hit anything anymore?*

Then a sound shrieked from Shingle's mouth, as if a demon had reached in with a clawed hand and wrenched it out of him.

Nate's smile returned. He got up and stalked, taking a circular route, swinging around to Shingle's right. *It's not over yet,* he reminded himself. Approaching with caution, Nate held his rifle ready.

Shingle did not see him coming He tried to crawl out of the black swamp water before he passed out and drowned in it. His right shoulder hung limp. He pulled himself another six inches with his bleeding left arm and caught Nate's movement. He tried to reach for a pistol, turning on his left side, but his right arm did not obey his will. Nate's bullet had finished it for good.

Nate fired into his chest, then again.

Shingle clutched his breast pocket where Nate's bullet entered as if it held a treasure he feared Nate might take from him. Blood flowed between his fingers. His chest convulsed with shallow, rapid breaths.

Nate always considered Shingle a hollow man. He could never find anything in his eyes except when angered or afraid or in pain. Most of the time he was just a deep pit of emptiness. Life ebbed from him, but Nate could not tell if he was nearly dead or if he was just a little less alive than he normally was. Nate put a bullet through his head to be sure.

Shingle lay in the mud, a disinterred body, a zombie with a rotting heart or no heart. Nate could not decide if he had done him a favor, then decided it did not matter. What did matter was he could do no more harm but stink up the woods for a while until the hogs ate him.

In Shingle's pack, Nate found personal items stolen from victims, mostly jewelry and money. There was little food and what there was came from the cache. He dumped everything out, keeping the food and ammunition. Nate retrieved a knife, some matches, and a lighter from Shingle's pockets. Anything that was not useful for survival he left on the ground. The pack, he tied to his, the rifle too.

When there is no way to buy replacements or supplies, taking items that can save your life from someone you killed in self-defense is not immoral. Nate eyed the jewelry and cash with distain and looked at Shingle's slack face. He seemed more at peace than Nate had ever seen him, but only a little less alive. *How many people suffered and died because you wanted that useless crap?*

Nate started for the farm, his steps lighter than before, a heavy burden lifted from his shoulders. There was no remorse, his soul had already turned the page, had already forgotten Chuckey Shingle. Too much had been wasted on him already.

Nate let the cow into the pasture and brought feed for it. Then he fed the chickens. Afterwards, he checked the barn for anything they may have missed when they packed everything to the cache. Entering the house, he checked every cabinet and drawer in the kitchen, finding a bottle of beer under the sink. He opened it and drank it with a simple meal of cold pork and bread, enjoying his last beer for a long time, perhaps the last beer he would ever drink. He was not much of a drinker, had never been drunk since he left the Army, but that beer tasted good for some reason.

Before leaving the house, Nate searched every inch, finding nothing of value but family photos. He put them in his pack, telling himself they were for Brian.

The cow stood in the field munching on brown grass as Nate headed back to the cache. There, he left both Shingle's and his own pack and headed straight for where Deni told him he would find the canoe. There was no sign of anyone else in the area, and he moved fast through the woods. The canoe was not hard to find with Deni's directions.

By late afternoon Nate was paddling upriver and past the farm; his pack, and Shingle's both loaded with food from the cache. They sat in the bottom of the canoe, tied in for safety in case of a capsize. He rounded a sharp bend, staying in the eddies and close to shore where the current was not so strong, and looked upriver to see smoke. A thin column rose straight up with no wind to push it sideways or disperse it in the treetops. It could be seen by anyone on the river in either direction.

Nate turned the canoe and slid its bow into the mud. After pulling it out of the water, he snatched his rifle up and entered the swamp.

Twenty minutes later, voices came to Nate's ears.

"Mommy, I'm hungry," A little boy said, his voice weak.

A woman touched his face gently with the palm of her hand as he lay on a blanket under a cedar tree. "I know, sweetheart. Daddy's trying to catch a fish to go with this rice I'm boiling." The boy's ribs showed under thin skin when he pulled his T-shirt up to scratch. The woman pulled the shirt back down, her eyes filling at the sight. "Keep your shirt down to protect against skeeters."

"It's the last we have. What about tomorrow?" A girl asked.

Nate came in close enough to see through the brush. There was a woman, about thirty, a boy, about five, and a girl Brian's age. The girl gathered firewood while the woman comforted the boy. The woman and girl were thin and weak also. The woman's eyes were sunken and without hope, but when she looked at her children they warmed with affection.

Their clothes were filthy and tattered and their bodies not much cleaner. It appeared they had been traveling a long time, perhaps months. *It must be bad if they prefer living like animals in the woods.* He remembered Deni and how she too was living in the woods and what she told them about the violence and lawlessness.

Nate went looking for the man. He found him throwing a cast net, pulling nothing out but weeds and the occasional shiner or small bream. A pump shotgun stood leaning against a tree ten feet from him. He was thinner than the rest of his family and obviously weak from starvation. A partially healed wound ran six inches down his left arm. It appeared to be a knife wound and had been closed with fishing line.

He needs to open that up and let it drain. It was red and oozing fluid.

Stepping from behind a hickory, his rifle ready, Nate spoke. "I have food."

The man dropped his net and lunged for his shotgun, tripping on a root and falling on his face in the mud.

"Don't touch that shotgun!" Nate warned. "I don't want to hurt you."

The man looked at Nate and then at the shotgun, just out of reach.

"Don't," Nate said.

Nate thought the man was still coiled to spring at the shotgun.

"Mr., I'm between you and my family," the man said.

Nate lowered the rifle slightly. "I don't want to hurt you or your family. They're hungry, I have food to spare. My farm is just downriver a ways."

The man's eyes involuntarily jerked towards his family back in the woods.

"They're fine. I didn't hurt them. And I won't. Stay away from that shotgun and I won't hurt you either."

The man seemed to calm down but was still suspicious. "You have food?"

"Yes."

"What do you want for it?"

"Nothing. I just don't want to be robbed or killed for my trouble. And for future consideration, if you want to travel unnoticed, don't build a fire in broad daylight."

The man rose slowly, backed from the shotgun, and said nothing.

Nate slowly walked to the shotgun and picked it up, keeping his rifle ready but not pointing directly at him. "Take what fish you got there, no need to waste it."

The man picked up the fish, his hands shaking.

"Calm down. I'm telling you the truth. I mean you no harm as long as you mean me none."

"You better not hurt them. Or I swear I'll take that rifle—"

"All right. We will leave your shotgun with your wife. If you want, you can come back with the food alone."

He stood there considering that but said nothing.

Nate thought he was calmer and perhaps starting to believe him. Obviously they had been through hell and trusted no one. "Let's go. I have a friend and son worried about me. I'm afraid they will come looking for me soon and want to get to them before that happens."

The man nodded. "If you are really helping, I thank you. All of us are starving."

"I noticed. The boy won't last much longer before he is past the point of no return without a stay in a hospital. And we both know that's not going to happen. Let me help."

They walked to the camp. The girl screamed when she saw Nate. The woman grabbed a butcher knife and kept her children behind her, her eyes wild with hate and fear. The little boy peered from around her hips, first one side and then the other, wild-eyed and shivering. All that was keeping the starvation weakened boy on his feet was abject terror.

Nate knew she would kill him if he let her get close enough with that knife. "Stay where you are. I'm not going to hurt anyone."

Her husband put his hands up. "It's okay! Drop the knife. He just wants to give us food."

"No way!" She said. "People don't give anything away anymore. He's lying."

Nate leaned the shotgun against a magnolia tree twenty feet from her, keeping his rifle ready and hoping he would not have to use it. "I'm going to take your husband to food. He will be gone about ten, fifteen minutes. Careful you don't shoot him when he comes back."

"I believe him. Stay here with the kids." The father's demeanor seemed to calm the mother.

Nate kept his eyes on all of them as he backed into the woods, the man off to his side.

"Where did you come from?" The man asked several minutes later as they walked.

"Our farm's not far from here. We've had so much trouble lately we left it."

The man stopped walking and turned to face him. "If you're abandoning it, maybe you will let us stay there."

"There isn't much left but shelter, a cow and some chickens."

The man's jaw dropped. "There are people out there who would kill you for just one egg. And you're leaving that?"

"It's too dangerous to stay," Nate said. "We have three good shooters. Two of us are ex-military. But we need more security to be safe there and work the farm."

"My wife and I can shoot well enough. We've both had to kill lately. My girl can stand watch as eyes and ears at least, and we're all hard workers. I mean, when we're not starving. Do you have what's needed to plant a crop?"

Nate felt new hope surge into him. He cocked his head, his eyes lighting up. "Yes."

"I assume your farm can produce enough food to feed us all."

"Easily," Nate said. "If someone doesn't come and kill us to take it."

The man smiled for the first time. "We're city people but we can work. I was in construction, mostly carpentry, but I can do just about anything that needs doing in construction. And we have toughened up a lot since everything went to hell. Just show us how to farm and we'll work from sunup to dark."

Nate said nothing more until they got to the canoe. "I tell you what, now it's your turn to prove to me you're trustworthy. When you're through recovering enough after a few meals, go upslope until you're out of the swamp. Just stay on the edge of the river valley and keep heading downriver and you'll come to my place. The field is way too large to miss, and you can see the house up on the hill. Can't miss it. It's got a tractor sticking halfway in the front."

The man looked puzzled.

"It's a long story. Like I said, we've had trouble too. The sickness took my wife and little girl, but my son and a friend are still alive."

"Sorry to hear that. For some reason we've had no problem with the plague at all; none of us have gotten sick. The trouble we've had is the crazies taking advantage of the chaos and the fact there is no food or much of anything else. We have money still, but all the looted stores are bare. And the gas stations have been drained dry by thieves who got the gas out of the underground tanks someway, so we had to abandon our car. Many stations burned down, whether by accident or arson, I don't know. Probably some of both. There is no power for the pumps, and the stations, like the stores, are closed anyway. There is no economy at all, and money is worthless. I haven't seen a cop in months, and you know what the result is."

Nate gave the man Shingle's backpack full of food. "That will hold you for a few days. You can stay at our place. It's kind of a mess, but it'll be a lot better for your family than camping in the woods. There's feed for the livestock. Take care of them and clean the house up a little. When we come to check, if you haven't killed the chickens and cow or taken anything but eggs, and used, but not abused, what little we left there, you will have taken a step towards earning our trust."

The man's eyes lit up. "Sounds like a deal. Together, both our families have a much better chance of surviving."

"I'm sure you can figure out how to milk a cow," Nate said. "Just remember to clean her udder first. You will contaminate the milk if you don't. There's a special soap in the barn for that. Clean the pail too."

"Thanks. My kids can use the milk."

"I will see you in two days. Keep that shotgun handy and stay alert. As far as I know, there's no one around at the moment, but we've had some come upriver from town and shoot my son, among other things. So be careful."

"We know about careful."

Nate smiled. "I noticed that. Better get back. Your family is worried."

"Yeah. Thanks for the food." He walked into the brush and disappeared.

Up ahead, the river branched and then reformed into one channel again. Nate paddled for the far side, keeping the island between him and the family as he went by. They were not the only ones experience had taught not to trust strangers. He would be an easy shot in that canoe, and he did not trust them completely yet.

Just perhaps, a friendship, a bond of trust, could be forged, and together, they could live on the farm and raise enough food for them all. Mel's supplies could keep them going if a crop failed or they could not work the field enough because of danger from marauders. They could repair the wall and there was enough steel plate and gas for the torch to make bullet resistant shutters to replace the wood ones. There might even be enough to make up a steel door or two. They could teach the girl to shoot and that would make six guns in a fight, enough to cover all sides of the house. Two standing watch would give them eight-hour shifts when there was no immediate danger.

Nate laughed at himself. *Don't get carried away. We will have to see. But just maybe...*

His heart swelled with renewed hope for Brian. The closer he paddled to Mel's retreat, the more he wanted to see him, wanted to tell him he was sorry. He wondered if Brian understood, if he would forgive him. He paddled faster. Maybe he could make it before dark.

The End

The following is the story of Nate Williams' grandparents as told to him by his father. This is a short story related to the novel in that it gives insight into where Nate gets his courage.

A REVOLUTION CALLED OFF

The middle-aged man's forehead beaded with sweat, though the afternoon temperature was in the mid-fifties. "It's warm for Montana this late in the year, isn't it?" He took a handkerchief out of a back pocket and wiped his face. "Mr. Williams, you're growing too much wheat. And you know it's a violation. If you don't destroy ten acres by next Saturday, I'll have to send some boys out here to do it. And…I'll have to fine you."

Jake Williams towered over him. His massive hands opened and closed, forming two hammers.

"I…I'm giving you a chance to get right with the law because of you being a wounded veteran and all."

Jake was silent for some eternal number of seconds. His chest rose and fell. His face was hard but calm. Then Jake's voice snapped the man straight. "First you trespass on my land while I'm at Sunday church with my wife, next you threaten to destroy my property and steal my money." Jake stepped closer. "Get off my land and don't come back."

The man rushed to his car and stopped with his hand on the door handle. "It's the law. It's no use you fighting it. You have exceeded your wheat quota and must—"

Jake took a step closer. "Leave. And don't come back or send anyone else out here."

The man barely got seated before he had the engine roaring and tires spinning, throwing dirt as he sped down the driveway.

"Who was that?" Jake's wife yelled from the kitchen window.

Jake's face suddenly softened. "He's from the government. Says I'm violating the wheat quota Roosevelt dreamed up some years ago. It was supposed to get us out of the Depression, or some such nonsense."

"You mean they can do that? Tell us how much feed we can grow on our own land? Wheat we need to feed our livestock?"

"Only if people let them. You start lunch yet?"

"Yeah."

"Well, I'll be in the barn working."

"Change out of your church clothes first."

"I won't get them dirty, Cath."

She started to say something, but he walked off to the barn.

Jake went straight to the back where he had a six-by-eight foot room he called his office. At one end was a small desk. At the other was a large beat-up old trunk. He stood on his toes and reached up over the top of a rafter and took down a key, then unlocked the trunk and swung the top open. There was a shoe box full of photos and letters.

He sat down at the desk and put the box in front of him. After removing seven envelopes, he pulled a letter out of one and read it.

Hey Jake. I hope this reaches you before you ship back to the States. I hear you caught one too. Thank God you didn't get it as bad as me. The boys wrote and said you'll be fine. I'm glad for you. You'll be sent home for a while though. That's what they said in their letters anyway. When you get back look me up. You know where I'll be.

And Jake, why haven't you written? I know. God damn it. It was not your fault. I'll be walking on pegs the rest of my life, but I'm alive.

You won't believe it, but I just got married a few weeks back. I remember you always bragging on your Cathy. Well, no offense, but I bet my Dora is prettier! We're happy. And the scars and legs don't bother her at all. I have you to thank for the life Dora and I are looking forward to.

If you ever need a peg-legged lawyer you got one, no charge. I'm not that busy right now anyway.

My practice will take a while to grow after me being over there nine months and then the year of recovery. Anyway, I wish you would write or call.

Take care of yourself, and let's pray the war is won before they send you back into that hell.

Jake swallowed hard and copied his friend's phone number from the letter on a piece of paper torn from a Sears catalog on the desk. After looking at a photo of a dozen men in dirty uniforms lined up and smiling with beard-shadowed faces for a few seconds, he put everything back in the trunk and locked it. He put the paper with his friend's phone number in his shirt pocket.

Cathy turned from the stove and looked Jake over when he walked into the kitchen. "Well, you didn't get your clothes dirty. How about that?" She went back to her cooking.

He rushed over, wrapped his arms around her from behind, and kissed her on the neck. "How about that?"

She kept a straight face. "How about what?"

He let her go and washed his hands in the sink. "I need to go to the supply store tomorrow, so I'll be getting up earlier than normal to get the chores done before I go."

"We just went day before yesterday."

"I want to call Tom, see how he's doing."

Cathy stopped short and turned to him. "Well. That'll probably be good for both of you."

Jake's chest rose and fell as he stood there looking at her. "Well, woman, are you going to let me starve? You'll never finish standing there looking pretty."

"If you get busy on the salad everything else will be done by the time you're through."

*   *   *

Jake hesitated before lifting the earphone.

"What now? We went all this way to use Sam's phone, now call him," Cathy said.

"There are things you don't know."

"That's because you won't tell me."

"Things you shouldn't know."

"Oh? Are you ashamed of what happened over there?"

"Of course not."

She brushed his hand lightly with hers. "Never mind me. It's none of my business. I think you should just call him though."

"Why don't you go have a look around while I do?"

She stifled a laugh. "At what? The feed sacks? The shovels? How about the rolls of barbwire?"

He just stood there and looked away, saying nothing.

"I'll wait in the truck."

When he walked out of the farm supply store she met him halfway. He put his massive arms around her and held her tight.

"He's coming here," Jake said.

He's coming to visit?"

"I asked him to."

"Good."

"He's bringing his wife. Wants to see if you're as pretty as her."

"I don't know as I like that. I'm no prize pig at the county fair, you know."

"Of course not. He doesn't mean any disrespect." Jake pulled away and turned from her to blow his nose on a handkerchief.

Her eyes watered. "When will they be here?"

"In a few days. He's dropping everything and bringing his associate with him."

"Associate?"

He turned and faced her. "I asked him for help."

"You mean that wheat quota nonsense is that bad? So bad you need a lawyer?"

"Not yet."

"If you don't start telling me what's going on, you and I are going to have a disagreement."

"I'm not going to give in to them, Cath. It's a little thing now, but it will escalate and get…Let's go home. I don't want to talk about it here."

*   *   *

Jake glanced at Cathy, sighed, and took another sip of coffee. "I appreciate you helping out on this, Tom."

Tom sat on a couch next to Dora and looked over the notice the man from the U.S. Department of Agriculture gave Jake.

Tom looked up. "Well, there it is: You are in violation of the Second Agricultural Adjustment Act of 1938. The evidence is that wheat out there. The guy is actually cutting you some slack. He doesn't have to give you a chance to plow the wheat under. He could have the wheat destroyed and you fined now. Either he's a decent man or he's afraid of you."

Cathy's eyes flitted from Tom to Jake. "He is not such a decent man, so it must be the later. He relishes his power over us little farmers."

"I only have until tomorrow anyway," Jake said.

"If I were you I would get out there and start plowing right now," Tom said. "You have about two hours before dark. Maybe you can ask a neighbor to bring his tractor and help you."

Jake shook his head slightly. "No. It's my land and my wheat and my sweat and Cathy's. If a man can't raise food to feed himself and his family on his own land, what are we fighting in Europe for?"

"You can't win. I didn't even bother to bring my associate after I researched case history on this law. There was a Supreme Court ruling less than two years ago, and the law was upheld and even strengthened. The era of constitutionally limited federal government is over. They can regulate anything and everything under the Interstate Commerce Clause. And I mean every part of your life, not just commerce. In fact, the ruling states that no commerce has to take place to fall under the Commerce Clause. Wickard v. Filburn, 317 U.S. 111 (1942). Filburn was the farmer."

"Who was Wickard?" Cathy asked.

Tom smiled. "The Secretary of the U.S. Department of Agriculture."

"What will happen if he doesn't destroy the wheat?" Cathy clasped her hands tightly.

"They will send people out here to plow it under, and you will be fined. It will be a hefty amount."

Jake spoke up. "That won't happen. They're not getting on my land again. And I'm not paying any fine. I'm all appreciative of the president's efforts to get us out of the Depression and through this war, but Roosevelt isn't God. And it was God that endowed all human beings with immutable rights. No government should be allowed to change that. This is our land. And what's on it is ours too. We work this land and it feeds us. We never asked for a thing from the government. And we ask for nothing now but to be left alone."

A wave of realization came over Tom's face. "I know what's on your mind, Jake, and I won't have any part of it."

"I never asked you to."

"You asked me for help."

"Yes, legal help. I do my own bleeding."

Cathy jumped out of her chair. "What are you talking about?"

Jake said nothing.

She turned to Tom. "You know what's happening. Tell me."

"I'm afraid he's going to get himself killed."

"What! The government is going to kill him over wheat?"

"No. Because of the same mule-headed stubborn streak in him that kept us alive over there. There were times when I think the enemy couldn't kill him because he simply was too stubborn to give them the satisfaction. Now he..." Tom noticed her face.

Dora, who had been sitting quietly until now, got up and put her left arm over Cathy's shoulders. "Nobody's killing anyone. You know how war veterans are, always talking rough."

Jake stood. "Cath, I won't live in a country where the government has no limits and a man has no rights. I saw it over there and I fought it. I'm not going to stop fighting it just because it's our own government."

Cathy shuddered. "No! Not over wheat! Or them trespassing on our land or your pride or anything. You came back to me, and I'm not going to lose you now. Not over wheat."

"It's not over wheat." Jake pointed out the window at the front yard. "That little sniveling paper pusher came up here and thought he would get his boots licked by someone who just spent more than a year in hell while he played with forms and enjoyed telling our neighbors when to jump and how high. It was spineless little desk jockeys like him who sent people to their deaths by the millions." Cathy's eyes widened. "Yes, by the millions. They don't tell you over here the half of it."

Cathy shook her head. "No. Whatever happened over there. No."

"They're going to send me back soon," Jake said. "Maybe I'll get the harvest in before, maybe not. They must have a thumping gizzard for a heart. To send men to die for other's freedom while they build up a government designed with thousands of default settings that result in good people losing everything: their property, their dignity, and their life. They think they know what's best for us. Well, the Nazis have their plans too."

"It's about your pride. I don't care what you say. It's just your pride. That little man made you mad. Well, go punch his lights out and get it out of your system. But don't go fighting the law just because someone made you mad."

"I already told you what it's about. I guess my words will never be enough. If you don't understand, I can't help it. You just won't understand. Either way, what's going to happen will be the same."

"What about me? You don't care?"

"You will have to stay in town until it's over."

"That's not what I mean."

"I know. And yes I do care. But I'm not going to go back to Europe to die after letting my own government heel me like a hound pup."

Cathy looked up at him. "There it is: your pride."

Jake pointed out the window. "We use that wheat to feed our livestock and bake bread. We don't even sell it. Until Tom just told us how it doesn't matter if there is any commerce or not, they still claim it's the commerce law or whatever, I was thinking Tom could tell them we don't sell it and they would leave us alone. Now I know even better than before that the law doesn't matter. They're going to run over us just the same." He shook his head. "I won't live like that. And I won't die like that. I will not go peaceably to the ovens. I learn fast. And I know there isn't much difference between a black uniform and a black suit."

Cathy blanched. "What do you mean by go to the ovens?"

Jake looked at Tom. "I wasn't supposed to talk about that. It just came out."

"Goddamnit! You better start opening up to me for once. I'm tired of you holding all the hurt in and letting it fester. Let it out. Lance it with words. Let the poison out so it can heal."

"Cathy. Watch your language."

She blinked. "Language? What about you? What's happening? I don't understand any of this. I want to know what's going on inside you. Tell me now."

"I'll tell you about the ovens, though I'm not supposed to."

"I want to know about you."

"No."

Her eyes filled. "What about the ovens?"

Jake walked to Cathy and led her to the other couch. "Tom, will you tell her?"

Tom motioned for Dora to sit beside him. "I haven't told Dora yet." He looked at her. "It won't be pleasant."

Dora forced a smile. "You were there, I wasn't."

"Our plane was hit by a fighter. The copilot was killed and the pilot badly wounded. He managed to keep it level long enough for most of us to jump before he passed out, or lost control of the plane. Anyway, most of our stick made it out. The others died in the plane. You know Jake, as big as he is, he's really too big to be a jumper. Hits the ground hard. But he has worked on his landing technique so much he manages to not break a leg or something."

Jake interrupted. "Tom, get with it, will you?"

"Okay, okay."

Tom shook his head. "We were way behind enemy lines and in deep...Jake saved our backsides many times. This is when he did things that got him written up for the Distinguished Service Cross. Lieutenant Anderson wanted to go one better. But higher-ups said no."

"Why didn't you just start with Hitler's invasion of Poland for God's sake?" Jake interjected.

"You're getting touchy in your old age, aren't you?" Tom smiled at the women. "Okay, Mr. Modesty, where was I?"

Jake's voice boomed. "You were about to tell them about the ovens, I hope. And be careful how you tell it. No need for melodrama or macabre stuff."

"Oh no, I wouldn't dare make a mountain out of a molehill. It's no big deal really, but I simply must embellish the story to keep my audience awake."

"That's not funny." Jake examined his shoes.

Tom became serious. "No, It's not. There's nothing funny about it. I'll never forget the stench of the mountains of skin-covered skeletons. And the smoke from the ovens. The human ashes falling from the sky like gray snow."

Cathy and Dora sat ashen-faced. Nothing was said for many moments.

Tom broke the silence. "It's ugly, but it's the truth. I expect the full story, or part of it anyway, will be released soon. They can't keep the lid on it forever."

"So you think that could happen here just because the government is telling us how much wheat we can grow?" Cathy asked Jake. "I think you're reacting to the horror of war and what you saw over there."

Jake stood and began to pace the room. "No, not for a long time. I mean it won't get that bad here anytime soon. I just know an unlimited, centralized government is dangerous. If we can't raise food on our own land to feed ourselves, what rights do we have?"

"I think Cathy is right," Tom said. "You're transferring your hatred and repulsion of what happened in Europe to America. I agree the government has stepped beyond the limits of the enumerated powers of the Constitution, but that does not mean our government is evil."

"People are people," Jake said. "Or do you think Americans are special and won't lower themselves to do such things? What about how the Negroes have been treated? And don't say it was just the South. You saw how they are treated in the Army even now. How many white soldiers have you heard say they won't take orders from a Negro officer? That they're only good for washing dishes? No. You can't count on Americans being different. Where did most Americans come from anyway? Europe. People are basically the same everywhere. Both the good ones and the bad ones—and the common ones somewhere in between."

"The government is just trying to do what's best for us. The wheat quota keeps the price up so farmers won't go broke." Dora looked around the room. "Isn't that true?"

"I'll give you that," Jake said. "I mean keeping the price up. But we're not selling the wheat. They're trying to force us to buy other farmers' wheat when we can grow it ourselves and keep the money. Is that right? Telling us what we can grow on our land for food is right? And what makes them think they know any better than anyone else what's best for us? Who gave them the right? The power? Tom admits it's not in the Constitution, so where did it come from? It does not exist. That's the answer."

"In the military officers take orders from their superiors and then carry them out, passing them down the ranks. Everyone follows orders," Tom said.

"That's the military," Jake said. "And it's necessary in time of war to use the system that works best to win because all of our rights are at stake if we lose. Individual rights are pushed aside to some degree out of necessity. In the civilian government it's different. Human rights—the individual—is supposed to be paramount. Also, officers are highly trained and tested in every way at every stage in areas that are important to being an officer. They prove their competence every day. All politicians have to do is get elected by being a better liar than their competitors."

"You're right there," Tom said.

Cathy's eyes filled. "They will send the sheriff or federal agents if you fight them. I can't believe you're thinking of fighting the law. You never break the law. Why are you going to risk getting killed? My parents are dead and Nate is off fighting. Now you want to leave me alone. You've been distant since you got back. I sometimes wonder if you still..."

"Cath..." Jake's eyes darted towards the front window. "Someone's coming up the drive."

Cathy stood and looked. "Looks like a government car."

Jake sighed. "It is. Army." His chest deflated.

Cathy saw his face. "What's wrong?"

Jake took three long steps and held her. "Lean on me, Cath. God made men bigger so their wives can lean on them."

"Are they here for you? Already?"

Jake swallowed hard and rested his chin on top of her head. "No. They're not here for me. I'm not due to report yet. And don't worry about what I've been saying. I'll plow the wheat under if it takes all night. Come on."

The two walked out on the porch together.

A man in uniform stood at the steps. "Mrs. Williams?"

"Yes." Cathy braced herself while Jake held her.

"I regret to inform you that your brother, Nate, was killed in action at—"

Jake took her in his arms.

Dora rushed to their side. The soldier stepped up on the porch and handed her a sheet of paper. "I'm sorry." He turned back to the car. "I hate this job."

Dora caught up with him. "You didn't kill him, tyranny did. Someone had to tell her."

Jake carried Cathy inside while Dora held the screen door open. The soldier in the olive drab car drove away.

Jake stopped in front of Tom. "Now all she's got is me." He carried her upstairs.

When he came down his face was wet. "She wants to rest a while. I'll go back up in a minute to check on her."

"I'm sorry," was all Tom could say.

Jake rubbed his hand across his forehead. "I didn't know him that well. It's her I'm worried about. Seemed like a good kid. Cath thought the world of him. I doubt if he was more than nineteen."

"You think I should go up?" Dora asked.

"No. I'll check on her in a minute. Then I've got to plow that wheat under. I don't want her worrying about me on top of this." Jake sat down across from Tom. "I have a favor to ask."

"Anything," Tom said.

"I remember one time you telling me your brother is a jeweler."

"Yes, he is. Need a ring for Cathy? You got it."

"No. Well, in a way, yes. I've got a Mason jar of gold coins put away. It's illegal to have them you know. Ten years and a big fine if they catch you with any gold coins or bullion. Part of the government's NRA or something. Anyway, I was wondering if your brother could melt those illegal coins down and turn them into legal jewelry. That way Cath can sell a ring occasionally to make ends meet. There's a little in the bank, and I send my Army pay to her, but that will stop if I'm killed. This farm's paid for, but that Mason jar of coins is all I can leave her in cash."

"Sure, my brother will do that. No problem. And I promise I'll help her out if you're not able to. I owe you that. It would be an honor."

Jake left them to check on Cathy. When he reappeared he was not alone. Cathy slowly walked to the bottom of the stairs and said, "I'm okay now. It's a little early, but I want to start dinner. It'll keep me busy." She turned at the kitchen door and smiled at them. "No more long faces. It's life—and the goddamn war." She put her hands up in front of her. "I'm fine. I got Jake." She went into the kitchen. Dora followed.

"Well, I must get busy plowing. You will have to eat dinner without me." Jake walked outside.

Everyone in the house heard the tractor as Jake headed for the field. Cathy watched through the kitchen window.

Four months later, the same young soldier came to notify Cathy, two months pregnant with Nate's father, that Jake was killed in action.

The End

An excerpt from my first novel

FEATHERS ON THE WINGS OF LOVE AND HATE: *LET THE GUN SPEAK*

By
John Grit

("Hoarse Whisperer" and "Shitwad" are temporary nicknames given to nameless characters who are Nazi-like national police officers trying to hunt down and kill a teenage boy in a Florida swamp.)

…"Damn! This creek seems to be more mud than water." Hoarse Whisperer took two more careful steps and found he was armpit-deep. But the water was not his problem at the moment, it was the fact he could not pull his boots out of the muddy bottom. He was already more than two feet into the sucking muck's clutches. Each time he put his weight on one foot to pull out the other, that foot would be pushed deeper into the swamp's sludge. Soon he was neck deep.

"Hey. Goddamn it. I need help!"

Silence.

"Come on now," Hoarse Whisperer yelled. "Don't be a shitwad."

"You should have known better than to try to cross that creek. I'm not going to get shot for you, dumbass. Chiang and Miles should be here soon."

"Bullshit. I'll be under in a minute. Get a rope or something."

"I don't have a rope. Maybe you can pull one out of your ass while we wait. Meanwhile, shut up. I can't hear if someone is walking up on me."

Five more minutes of soaking and sinking was all Hoarse Whisperer could take. The boy heard his voice lose all façade of courage. "I'm going under! Get me outahere now!"

Silence, but for the rumble of distant thunder.

"Pleeease help me. I don't want to drown in this goddamn mud."

A barking squirrel in a live oak forty yards away answered him. The man behind him remained silent.

"Come on," Hoarse Whisperer said. "Get me out of here. That boy's either dead or gone I tell you. Otherwise he would've shot me by now."

The boy watched the man's head bobbing over and around his scant cover, a small scrub oak. "Come on Shitwad," he breathed. "What's to think about? I'm just a Southern white trash farm boy. What do I know about an ambush?"

Shitwad took one last careful look across the glade. "Hold your shit together while I find a pole or something. I guess you're right. The boy is gone."

Now standing on the edge of the creek, Shitwad observed, "You're not that far out. Just stretch your carbine out this way, and I'll pull you out. There aren't any poles handy anyway."

Hoarse Whisperer turned at his waist as much as possible and pointed his carbine at Shitwad.

Shitwad jumped to his left. "Asshole. Now you're going to shoot me. Give me the butt end if you want me to pull you out."

Hoarse Whisperer glared over his shoulder. In silence, he simply turned his rifle around and held it out by the barrel.

Pulling only forced the stuck man under water.

"The angle is wrong," Shitwad said. "I'm pulling too horizontally. And with you facing away from me, pulling on the carbine just pulls you over backwards."

Each time they tried it, he came up spiting and gasping for air. "Enough. You're going to drown me, goddamnit."

"Look what happens when I leave you two alone."

Shitwad nearly fell over until he saw it was Robert who had just walked up on them. He caught his breath, putting his left hand to his chest as if he thought he was having a heart attack. "Oh shit Chiang. I could've shot you."

Looking incredulous and pulling himself back on his heels with a smug sneer on his face, Robert said, "Bullshit. If I were the boy I could have shot you." He glanced around and asked, "Where are the others?"

At that instant, a bullet entered and exited Robert's head. Pink mist exploded from his skull, and he fell on his face in the mud.

Shitwad opened his mouth wide in shock and horror one second before he too fell dead at the creek's edge, his head half submerged in the coffee-black water. Crimson gouts of blood spurted for a few seconds, spreading onto the wet mud as his one eye visible above water stared blankly at Hoarse Whisperer's back. Miniature wavelets produced by Hoarse Whisperer's shaking lapped in and out of his half-open mouth.

Hoarse Whisperer forced himself to turn at the waist and neck and look over his right shoulder to see if what he feared had happened. "Oh shit!" He unloaded in his pants.

Waiting for another target, the boy guessed forty minutes had passed. The slight breeze of early afternoon, generated by a coming thunderstorm, gradually shook off its lethargy, exciting the green leaves of tree and bush to dance with more vigor. He lifted his nose. A trace of ozone wafted to his nostrils. Cooler air from high above washed over his face, drying some of the sweat beading on skin.

The squirrel in the live oak, encouraged by the recent silence, resumed a timid barking, soon turning into a chastising scold of things in general. Myriads of frogs croaked and bullied silence into partial submission with their monotonous love songs. Thunder, paled by distance, hung in the heavy air for a moment and faded to a weak hint of distant storms.

Hoarse Whisperer had sunk several more inches into the creek bottom. He could smell the swamp before, but now the very lifeblood of this quaking liquid land was only three inches under his nostrils. Eons of frequent rains had washed everything of flora or fauna that had lived and died and rotted to be reabsorbed by the liquid land from which it came into the creek. The after-smell of life and death, that which is temporary fermented and distilled into that which is forever; the quintessence of ever-present mortality permeated his overloaded senses. He smelled his own death. His face was deathly white, and he was shivering violently, his teeth chattering, though the water was bathtub-warm.

Farther back in the woods, someone was trying to quietly sneak closer but not having much luck with his intentions of stealth. The boy continued to listen and watch, his lucent form still immersed in the green gloom of the jungle, now under the shade of heavy rain clouds and tossed ever more violently by the winds.

Hoarse Whisperer's ears discerned the rasping impact of someone moving through palmettos from the wind-tossed treetops and brush colliding in the gathering commotion. He yelled, "Miles, come help me. I'm drowning."

There was crashing in the brush and a blur of motion. Miles stopped behind a hickory tree. The voluminous midsection of his sweat-soaked body was exposed on each side of the inadequate tree trunk.

Miles timidly pulled his head out from around the hickory just enough to look at the back of Hoarse Whisperer's shivering head poking out of the water. His skin tingled with nervous tension, all senses on high-volume intensity, eyes funneling in and focusing the images before him in minute detail. He saw a two-foot-long water moccasin swimming upstream towards the head. Hoarse Whisperer's palpable terror and helpless state permeated the air, eroding much of Mile's intestinal fortitude. A suffocating feeling there was not enough oxygen in the atmosphere came over him.

The boy could see his eyes, and his eyes told him Mile's mind was slogging through a miasma of confusion…

…Clouds that had rolled in earlier were building fast now, high and deep under the energy of the sun. The humid air could take in no more moisture. It started to rain, but stopped after a few minutes. A surge of wind, mixing hot air with cool, came down from the darkening sky and swept them without warning. The roar of a soaking downpour rolled across the woodland in an advancing sheet and hit all at once. In seconds, Miles and the boy were nearly as wet as Hoarse Whisperer. The crack of a lightning bolt assaulted their ears and set Hoarse Whisperer's bowels moving again. He moaned and looked about wild-eyed.

Already, the blood of those fallen soaked into the soil, and the boy's arm painted the ground crimson where he lay. As it continued to rain, the blood of the living and the dead washed into the creek. Soon, only God would know the blood of the oppressed from that of the oppressor.

Miles said nothing. There had been gunfire multiple times earlier; this was no time to take chances. Carefully, he pulled his head out a little so he could see more to the left. A bolt of lightning struck nearby. He franticly pulled his head back behind the tree. Regaining his composure somewhat, he timidly brought his head slowly out in the open and peered into the streaming slant of the downpour, shivering in the cold rain.

The bark of the boy's Garand reverberated among the trees and slowly faded into the drenching atmosphere. Miles lay on his back, carbine lying across his chest, eyes staring blankly at boiling storm clouds above.

The wind and the rain continued.

The boy heard them talking. He knew Miles was the last. Still, he did not go carelessly to the creek. He took his time. There was no hurry. Why not make use of every advantage you have? There is always one more thing you can do to put the odds in your favor. Never take unnecessary chances.

He wanted this last one to see his hate before he died, to know why he hated them, to feel something of the value he placed on the two they murdered without thought or feeling. He might as well know before he goes to hell.

There was no way to tell how long the boy's face had been there watching him slowly drown. He was just there, or his face was, as if he had just emerged from the dripping wall of green as an alligator comes to the mirror surface of a bayou.

His impassive face contrasted with the heat of his eyes. They dominated his face, leaving no room, no capacity for emotion, all emotion in the eyes. They were too old for a young face. The heat of hate stared straight through the drowning killer and a thousand yards beyond at something hideous, visible to the boy only. It would chill anyone who felt it. But the boy was unafraid. He was past fear, past pain, past mercy. He had run all such things into the ground and left them far behind, gasping and dying, ran to death by force of will.

The boy was dead. In his place was born a wild creature of a primordial past, the green gloom of the woodland's trackless wilderness his environing haunt. The boy had relinquished himself completely to the shadow that had followed him all his life. The shadow had merged with the boy. They were one now.

In his heart lived the Human Spirit, the cumulative product of centuries of lives lived and lost, births and deaths, arisen from the smoke of long ago campfires by the echoes of past drumbeats.

Hoarse Whisperer closed his eyes. The water was now above his mouth, forcing him to breathe through his nose. The sucking in and exhaling of air through his nostrils against the intimately close surface of the water was the only sound he heard above the gentle patter of rainfall in the endless liquid stillness of time.

When he reopened his eyes, the face was gone.

18537666R00099

Made in the USA
Lexington, KY
10 November 2012